TALKER

RON KENYON

Tellwell Talent
www.tellwell.ca

ISBN
978-0-2288-3521-9 (Paperback)
978-0-2288-3522-6 (eBook)

PART 1

AS IT WAS

CHAPTER 1

I'm not there, I'm gone! What the fuck?

Dell felt tightness penetrate his whole body, a kind of deep anxiety, and panic. Desperate, he couldn't think. She was *gone*; he was unable to connect to his avatar, Kata, who he deeply identified with. She was everything to him.

He turned everything off—it had to be an error, a bug, something like that—it couldn't really be *happening*. He waited 20 seconds, counting each one … *15, 16, 17, 18 …* Then he slowed his pace … *19 …* 20 … before rebooting. As he waited for the compute to fire up, he took long, slow breaths, trying to calm down; but he couldn't relax. His breath remained short and fast. He felt like he was going to have a heart attack.

Calm down, he told himself. Then he turned everything on again. *It was only a glitch, probably just a power outage.* But when everything was turned back on, there was still no Kata.

He sat up and blinked in disbelief. He started
searching his hard drive for an archived file so he
could recreate her ... but there was no trace of her,
no history—nothing. She was gone, nonexistent.
'Otherlife', the site where his avatar, Kata, existed
was still there—as was sister site 'Afterlife'—but Kata
wasn't. This left Dell with no entry into these digital
worlds. He'd been completely eliminated from these
places, he felt he belonged.

What can I do, he wondered; *where can I connect to
get her back?* There had to be a site somewhere where
he could log on and prove that he was Dell and Dell
was Kata—and that Kata was totally integrated in the
Otherlife site.

Think ... how was it that he became Kata? He
remembered the online entry forms; he remembered
clicking on the 'I agree' boxes. Somewhere, there was a
record of that. He cursed himself for not keeping track.
He *had* to be able to get his Kata identity back. She was
an important part of him. Kata was somebody—*more*
than somebody. At least he felt that way.

Dell was a young male-identified human who, like
many in the city in which he lived, worked for The
Organization, part of the governing system. Most
often just referred to as 'the Org', this conglomerate not
only monitored daily 3D life, but set up and oversaw
the digital afterlives and otherlives that Dell had so
unexpectedly found himself shut out of.

In his 3D life, Dell, had a normal life, living in a standard condo, eating, drinking, going out for walks from time to time, and maybe having a meal with friends who knew him only as Dell, not Kata. These 'real life' friends had their own online personas as well. Sometimes their 3D lives and their digital lives intersected; more often they did not.

Dell ate, slept, and paid his bills, but Kata lived a life with meaning—she had friends, relationships, and a *purpose*—which was to evolve as a persona in harmony with the goals and beliefs of the Otherlife, to develop, and to have a defined meaning.

His purpose was being Kata; without her, he was nothing.

There must be a way of getting her back, he thought. *There must be a way of getting back into the program.* All the things he loved to do in life were online, and now he was not. Over time, Dell had allowed his 3D life to diminish until he had only a minimum presence—the basics. What would he do without Kata?

His stress turned to paranoia, taking his imagination to all kinds of places. *What happened to Kata? Was she hacked? Was it because I did something wrong, or had her do something wrong and so the Org revoked my online privileges? Why is this happening?*

He knew the Org sometimes revoke privileges to Afterlife and Otherlife—but why had *his* privileges been revoked? Had her identity been stolen from him? Was someone else now Kata?

The Org made it clear to all citizens that online identity theft was a capital offense and the penalty was to be forever banished from Otherlife and Afterlife, plus a period of house confinement in the 3D world. Dell had thought this harsh until now; now he wished the worst for whoever was responsible for this.

He felt like the best part of him was missing. Where Dell had a fixed and dead-end life, his avatar, Kata, would go on forever. Kata's database was hundreds of time larger than Dell's—she would continue building, developing, and participating in Otherlife long after Dell was gone.

Dell left his condo. He had to get out and walk so he could stop obsessing. He needed to escape. He decided a drink would be good and so he headed toward a nearby bistro.

As he walked down the perfectly groomed streets, maintained by the Org, he studied the faces around him, wondering if anyone else had ever had this happen. Were there others who had suddenly had their meaningful digital lives ripped from them and their avatars kidnapped? It was impossible to tell. Unused to reading real human emotions, he couldn't see other's distress, so presumably they couldn't see his? Besides, nobody looked at him. Facial recognition was becoming a lost art as more and more people retreated to their online lives.

He entered the bistro. He'd only been here once before. He considered it a hangout for losers, a place where people with tech and other challenges congregated; however, today he felt like a loser himself, so he felt like this was where he belonged.

The bistro was almost empty. He sauntered over to a window table where he could watch people pass by on the street. A waitress soon joined him. "What would you like today, dear?" she asked with a smile that seemed genuine. Dell immediately felt better—or at least not out of place.

"A beer, please. IPA, make it a pint," he said. Then he decided to go all out. "Could I also have some peanuts?" he asked.

Normally he would never order peanuts; they were banned from most places—but not these bistros. He remembered how much he had once liked them. He was pretty sure he wasn't allergic.

"Certainly, right away. Salted or tamari?" asked the waitress with even a bigger smile.

"Tamari is good."

Dale drank a first pint of beer, then another, while slowly consuming the peanuts. The smooth, cool taste of the beer and its slight bitterness contrasted sharply with the salty, crunchy peanuts. He concentrated on the tastes as the alcohol took effect. Beer and peanuts—who ever invented that combination? It was a perfect way to relieve the panic and anxiety.

Looking around at the losers, misfits and non-techs who were populating the bistro as he sat, he thought, *some of them probably don't even have avatars.* Few of them were checking mobiles. He doubted they even had them.

He smirked. At least he had a mobile … but he didn't have Kata. A chill ran down his spine as he tried to block the thought.

At the back of the bistro, a group of people were playing some instant gratification machine. *Didn't that used to be called pinball,* wondered Dell?

Next to him, a group of three oldsters were chatting back and forth about something. Two older men, one in a wheelchair, and a greying woman, seemed to be enjoying the noise they were making. The woman cackled at something the man in the wheelchair said, an annoying noise that Dell wasn't used to as he spent most of his time online. They were of an older generation who hadn't evolved, people who had refused to adapt to the digital world the Org had created for the citizens of the world.

Dell listened, trying to get the gist of what they were on about. They jumped from subject to subject, and he soon realized they spoke with various degrees of irreverence towards authority, and often made jokes about the Org.

After a while, Dell he heard the conversation switch. He heard the woman explaining her 'talker' service to the others. Once or twice a week, a person came by her apartment and spent two hours with her, just talking.

That was such an unusual thing that it interested Dell. He paid closer attention.

"What do you talk about?" asked the man in the wheelchair. He was wearing a protective helmet, as required by the Org for people his age, and his long grey hair and beard poured out of it, covering most of his face. Dell smiled to himself. *It must be difficult to get digital facial recognition on the guy,* he thought as he glanced at a camera in the corner of the room.

The woman smiled, "Anything and everything," she said. "The service is provided by the Org for people who have a disorder, or a challenged classification. They say face to face contact with other humans is good for us."

"Kind of like we're doing now—like people used to do before Otherlife and Afterlife were created?" the wheelchair man asked with a tinge of sarcasm. They all laughed.

"Yes, just like that," said the woman. "Like the old days, which only old folks like us remember or appreciate. People these days have their heads in their mobiles. They don't know how great it is to share a laugh in real time."

"Is that talker program like the program they had for pet birds?" asked the other man. Physically, he was the opposite of the wheelchair man, who carried so much weight it made him look like he was literally spilling out of his wheelchair—he was so skinny he looked lost in his chair.

"No, it's another one," the woman said. "You can have both. I had both until he died."

"The talker?"

"No, the bird. It was a male bird."

How weird is it that they're discussing talkers? thought Dell. He'd been receiving notices in his inbox on job opportunities as a talker. He hadn't paid much attention—it seemed like just an Org job just like any other, and it offered nothing to stir the imagination—but now his interest was piqued.

He knew the 'talker initiative' was part of a new offline, outlook-enhancing social cohesion policy. And he knew they were insistent with their recruiting efforts. For some reason, they seemed personally interested in *him*; but then again, everything was personally targeted these days. It all had to do with algorithms and computer usage. Like everyone else, he was being tracked, his personality traits monitored.

Dell started thinking. With no more online life, no Kata to slip into, maybe it was time for a change. It could be some time before he sorted out what had happened and got his online life active again. Perhaps it wouldn't be a bad idea to try to fill the void with a new job. It wouldn't hurt to apply. He was qualified; his current position of receptionist/information officer would be considered a training credit for the higher-paying talker job...

Dell's wheels started turning. He had paid little attention to the recruitment notices, and had deleted them as soon as he'd received them. But now things had changed. In his 3D job, the only thing that motivated him was all the time he got to spend online as Kata while he went through the motions of forwarding public enquiries to an AI system. Now that was not available to him, and with the loss of his online life, he had no motivation or purpose. There would be no stimulation until he got Kata back. *What the hell,* he thought. *I should apply to be a talker. What do I have to lose?*

He had never felt the need for offline conversation and he wasn't sure he would be any good at it—but how hard could it be? Kata had been a good conversationalist; he would try to remember how she did it.

CHAPTER 2

The room Dell found himself in as he waited for an interview for the talker job was just like many other rooms Dell had waited in during his employment with the Org. The walls were off-white, the flooring was simulated oak and a series of plastic chairs lined the wall. There was some shelving featuring pamphlets, some magazines and some literature on 'the art of conversation', as well as documents outlining the rules and regulations applying to the job of talker.

Dell thought it odd that there was so much paper in the Org office, as they constantly emphasized non-use of paper, and the importance of staying digital. *Are they trying to encourage the anti-digital, pro-paper activists,* he wondered?

A nod to technology could be seen on a screen on the wall that had a video discussing the 'do's and don'ts' of the talker job running in a loop. There was also a slogan that kept popping up on the video, one Dell had seen in the notices for the talker job he had received in his inbox. It said: *Offline Participation Makes Online Life Richer.*

Dell picked up a pamphlet entitled, *Understanding Before Replying* and thumbed through it. It said that people formulate ideas about subjects before they hear the explanation—even when it is something they know little or nothing about. Dell wasn't sure about that, but he read on. The pamphlet further said that a talker needed to listen in order to understand what the other person was trying to communicate. "Do not respond with your own ideas," it said. "Talkers are to guide a conversation, and their job is to keep the person they are speaking with feeling positive—but they are to do so using the participant's words, not their own."

This wasn't the first time Dell had been exposed to these ideas. He had read, heard, and seen communication to this effect on videos and billboards and understood that, while effective talking was therapeutic for some, you had to know and apply certain precautions to ensure a conversation was comfortable and acceptable for both parties.

There were four other people sitting in the waiting room with Dell, presumably waiting for the same interview; another male-identified person and three female-identified ones … or at least Dell *thought* that was how they identified. Three were face down in their mobiles and one was wearing large slim goggles, so it was difficult to tell from facial features which way they swung. None of them even looked up when Dell entered, and no one besides Dell was checking out the pamphlets.

Their lack of awareness made Dell a little uncomfortable about the idea of navigating the 3D world in such a robust way, and, as he thought of Kata's loss, a familiar sense of panic came back along with a new feeling of having been victimized. *All the people in this room except me probably have their avatars intact and are in their programs right now,* he thought. *They could care less about changing jobs.* None of them seemed nervous about the job interview, that's for sure. It's just as he would have felt a short time ago.

How many of us will actually be hired, he wondered? He'd heard there was a growing need for talkers, so he thought maybe they would all get through the interview. All of them had made it through the first and second rounds of testing, or they wouldn't be here right now.

One thing about the job that appealed to Dell was that, unlike some jobs with the Org, having an avatar was not a requirement of the talker job. The job was about dealing with the 'challenged'—the aged and non-techs—and many of them had never been online in their lives. He knew how wonderful it was to be Kata, navigating the breathtaking, online world of Afterlife. He couldn't imagine how these poor souls managed to get through their depressing, humdrum days. *The challenged have the right to wellbeing, too,* he thought, *and that's why they need talkers.*

Studies had shown that communicating face to face prevented anxiety and was effective for treating social disorders. Old-fashioned cognitive behavior therapy was back—or so it was suggested by the Org.

Dell had prepared for this interview. It had taken two one-hour online sessions and one 20-minute offline session with a consultant who specialized in the talker trade to do so. As he learned about the job, he was surprised to find that being a talker was becoming increasingly important to him. It felt good to have a purpose in his 3D life. He'd toiled away as a receptionist for far too long. And while he missed his exciting online life as Kata, he'd come to accept that he had to make the most of his offline time.

"Good and effective communication requires the right usage of all the senses," the consultant had told Dell, adding, "Intonation and expression are more important than word choice."

He had watched videos on body language, studying its underlying meanings and how to use it to become more effective in communicating. He'd learned that, as a talker, he would start with one-on-one conversations and eventually move up to group conversations.

In the interview, he would need to prove his interactive and interjective skills matched with his body language.

The door opposite his seat opened and a young female-identified person in her late twenties walked out. She had short hair, cut in a crewcut, and was dressed much like Dell, in a T-shirt, vest, jacket and tight cords. Dell noticed that, like him, she was slightly pudgy around the waist. This was not unusual; all but one of the others waiting for an interview were able to conveniently rest their mobiles on their protruding stomachs—an obvious advantage. His parents had told him that, in the past, people were often judged by appearance, and that obesity was considered a problem—but this was before the word 'obese' was banned, 'taking your place with space' became the mantra, and 'weight enhanced' became the politically correct term.

However, while the Org still pushed exercise and a healthy lifestyle, the importance of healthy living was becoming hard for most people to understand, as online existence was generally far more interesting than offline life. There seemed to be no reason to maintain the earthly shell—except, of course, to deal with basic bodily needs. Further, the Org had to be careful to about its wording in publicity campaigns to get people moving and eating their vegetables. Targeting specific groups, such as the weight challenged, was offensive and might bring a shit-storm of disapproval.

After losing Kata, one of the hardest aspects of living offline, Dell discovered, was that nobody seemed to know you existed. He started seeing a therapist about it, and he told Dell this was probably why Dell was attracted to being a talker. "It is your way of combating apprehension and anxiety," the therapist told him. Dell did not tell the therapist he had lost his online persona, but this analysis made a lot of sense. Losing Kata was like losing his best friend and a piece of his soul at the same time. It certainly had made him anxious.

"Dell Gabo," called out a voice from inside the adjoining room.

Dell stood up and stepped as confidently as he could toward the room. Once inside, he noticed immediately that it was brighter than the waiting room—one wall was completely windowed. A large conference table stood in the middle of the room and at the far end sat two definite males of an older generation and a female-identified, slightly younger. All of them were dressed in the latest managerial style, and the two men might have taken their clothes from the same closet. Dell knew it would be difficult to remember which was which after the interview; only their ethnic roots differentiated them, as one had slightly darker skin.

He wondered at this. It was often hard for Dell to remember offline personas, as he spent so little time looking at people's faces; then again, up until now there had been little need to.

"Could you have a seat, Mr. Gabo—it is Dell Gabo isn't it?" the woman asked.

"Yes, Dell Anthony Gabo."

"How are you today, Dell Anthony?" she further asked.

"Very well, thank you. I've been looking forward to this interview, and the chance to join your team, ever since I received the invitation to apply. I'd like to thank you for this opportunity."

"You're very welcome," continued the woman. "My name is Gabriela Smith. This is Timothy Wang, and Benoit Fortin," she said, indicating the two men.

Dell nodded greetings to the two men. Ms. Smith said, "Make yourself comfortable. As you have probably guessed, we have some questions for you." She looked at the slightly darker man. "Mr. Wang, would you like to begin?"

"Yes," said Mr. Wang. "Mr. Gabo, I have several questions for you. First, what interests you about becoming a talker? Second, as a talker, how do you see your role in The Organization, and society in general. And third, Mr. Gabo, what is the greatest attribute you will bring in your role as a talker?"

Dell sat upright, clasped his hands together on the table in front of him chapel style (as his consultant and the body language videos had suggested), and said, "I like to converse with people, and I like to encourage others to express themselves and to communicate. I believe strongly in the talker mandate—to provide face to face contact and a full sensual experience ..." He caught himself quickly with the misuse of words and said, "… I mean, experience of the senses."

Noticing no reaction at his faux pas, he went on, "I also consider myself to be a good listener. I *enjoy* listening, and I've put a lot of effort into learning to listen effectively. I understand that some people have pent-up anxiety that needs to be expressed and they can only express it if they feel someone is actually *listening.*"

He saw Wang nod slightly, so he added, "And my greatest attribute is my belief in the Organization's role in maintaining and advancing the wellbeing and security of all."

"I see that you've watched the Dr. Epstein video," interjected Mr. Fortin dryly. "What is your opinion, or should I say how do you *feel* about his premise that the best way to relieve anxiety and other personality disorders is through avatar transfer online? In other words, choosing a persona *without* those disorders, because, as he states, 'offline and online grow together'?"

At this question, Dell was instantly reminded of the loss of Kata and he wondered if his slight tinge of anxiety about being avatar-less was noticeable. He took a deep breath and answered, "I believe what Dr. Esptein states is true for 90 percent of us, and I agree 100 percent with what he says … but there is still a place for offline, face to face communication—and talkers provide an important service in this regard.

Not everyone has adapted to digital or quantum lives. Some still live mostly, or entirely, offline, for example the tech challenged and tech resistant."

Fortin nodded slightly, and Dell continued, "Dr. Epstein speaks of the importance of offline-online adjustment. As talkers, we must deal with offline adjustments and, if successful, we can reduce offline anxiety and increase offline wellbeing."

Fortin frowned and asked, "What does antagonistic feedback mean to you?"

Dell was thrown off guard by the word 'antagonistic'. He had trained for, and rehearsed, a myriad of questions and answers and so far the interview felt as if they were all reading from the same script. However, his trainer had prepped him, telling him they might rapidly change the subject to test his inner true beliefs and ethical values.

"If a person is committed to a set of values, those values will be deeply entrenched in their neurological make-up, and there will be little or no hesitation when they answer a question," he told Dell. "Their true values will always reveal themselves."

Dell had contemplated his true values over and over, but the word 'antagonistic' threw him. He had recently discovered a well of resentment with regard to the loss of Kata, and was feeling antagonistic himself. He recovered quickly though, remembering what he'd learned. He had to adopt the right body language to answer the question.

He leaned forward slightly as he said, "I believe in adapting to the personality of the client, and their wellbeing has to be my focus. Disagreement can be positive if it leads to better communication, but generally an antagonistic attitude is counterproductive. Pushed to an extreme, it can even lead to serious antisocial behaviour."

Fortin seemed to be eating up his words, so he added, "I believe Dr. Epstein says that one must *guide*, not oppose. Antagonistic behaviour is opposing for the sake of opposing—it doesn't lead to a higher level of understanding. It's what he calls a 'contrarian personality disorder'. Talkers need to be less concerned about making points or winning arguments, and *more* concerned about reaching understanding."

He could tell by the way they were looking at him that the interview was still on track. As long as he wasn't obliged to elaborate about his avatar, he felt it would be okay.

He ventured, "I strongly feel that a good talker can create dialogue in a safe, secure manner and lead people to see that diversity of opinion is socially enhancing, that we can argue in a positive, constructive way. There can be no wellbeing without a sense that we can disagree yet continue to converse. Safety and security is paramount. As talkers, we must keep this in mind."

He watched their eyes. Ms. Smith would be the one to decide his fate—he could feel that. The others in the room were careful not to contradict her and tended to show deference to her; at least that's what he observed. As the interview panel looked at their notes, he discreetly studied her. She had a strong physical presence. She was tall and slim, more female than male and had a somewhat transgender appearance. All her traits, masculine and feminine, seemed to meld together into perfection, as if she had been cloned for authority.

There was no doubt about it; she scared the living shit out of Dell—and probably Mr. Wang and Mr. Fortin as well.

"Well, Mr. Gabo," Ms. Smith said, looking up from her notes, "I think we have enough information for us to assess your abilities as a talker. If chosen, you do realize the immense responsibility you will have towards your participants? Many don't have the assets and good fortune most of us have. Some might even be a little hostile toward you and reject your recommendations and actions."

Dell nodded. "I understand," he said.

She added, "Remember, they are not 'clients' or 'beneficiaries', but 'participants'. It is important that you chose the correct term when speaking to, or of, them. Words are not neutral—they send messages, positive and negative. 'Client' and 'associate', for example, give a commercial, transactional connotation to the relationship. We do not use those words."

Dell nodded again.

Ms. Smith paused and stood up. Her colleagues followed suit, and Dell did as well. To conclude, Ms. Smith said, "Remember, as a talker your job is to reassure your participants. This may entail ensuring them about the program *itself*. Not all of them think face to face communication is beneficial, so it's up to you to talk about the benefits of the talker program. You also have the obligation of keeping us abreast of anything you discover that could jeopardize either the wellbeing of your participants, or the reputation of the program. Also, while many are tech challenged, some of them have active online lives, which are generally more exciting to them than their *offline* lives.

"They prefer virtual life to real life?" asked Dell. He understood. He did too.

"Yes," said Ms. Smith, "But for your information, Mr. Gabo, those terms—'virtual life' and 'real life'— 'have been rendered obsolete. The Organization has decided to get involved in online existence to regularize it, ensure quality control and make the experience of transition between the two seamless. We prefer the terms 'bounded' and 'boundless'."

"So, 'bounded' means real life and 'boundless' means Afterlife and Otherlife?" asked Dell.

"Yes," she said.

"Did you create Afterlife and Otherlife?"

"Yes, the Org created these boundless realities," she said. "Mr. Fortin, here, is our historical specialist. Perhaps, Mr. Fortin, you can explain?"

"Certainly, Ms. Smith," Fortin said obediently. "It all began when it became obvious that the virtual world was, shall we say, a little chaotic. There were competing philosophies, world views, religions and belief systems, and violence was common. To address this, some of the world's best thinkers got together and determined that people needed some type of existence outside themselves, a place where the playing field was leveled so resentment and discontent could be abolished—a version, perhaps, of the fabled Heaven. For some, an added benefit to this concept is that, through an avatar, they could continue after their earthly demise, perhaps for all eternity."

Dell nodded. He was at least marginally aware of the reasons that Afterlife and Otherlife were created.

Fortin went on, "In the beginning, there was only Afterlife and it was based on the basic belief systems of the time. We took Christians, Muslims, Buddhists, Hindus, Rastafarians, Druids, etcetera—all the recognized belief systems—and integrated them into two main swim-lanes according to whether or not a deity was involved. This worked for a while, but soon the need for more diverse forms of the same thing arose. That's why today, in the Christian program alone, we have versions of Heaven ranging from Number 2 to Number 9. Before you ask, the reason we had to eliminate Number 1 was so it didn't indicate any kind of pecking order. You know how people get!"

Despite himself, Dell smiled. He *did* know. Right at that moment, he was hoping *he* would be 'number one' and get the job.

Fortin went on, "This worked well and so we copied it into the other Afterlife belief systems. Soon, the Afterlife system was incredibly popular. However, in short order the Atheists, Agnostics, and science-based were crying foul because a government funded program as only catering to people who believed in deities, and so, to make a long story short, we created Otherlife to address their beliefs."

When he finished speaking, Ms. Smith asked, "Does that satisfy your curiosity Mr. Gabo?"

"Yes, Ms. Smith, and thank you, Mr. Fortin—I never knew the history behind Afterlife and Otherlife."

"And now you do," concluded Ms. Smith. Then she formally ended the interview by saying, "If you are selected you will have a month of training and an opportunity to accompany another talker to get the feel of it. It is important to remember, Mr. Gabo, that we all work as a team for the benefit and wellbeing of our participants. Good luck."

CHAPTER 3

Seen from a distance, it was breathtaking. A fine white mist covered the place and stretched out as far as the eye could see. The buildings were pure white and sparkling, gold spires rose up from the mist here and there. What looked like silver comets traversed the skies above and, every now and then, an explosion of sparkling light fell down over the spires. This was Afterlife, a place of extreme beauty ... more specifically, this was Heaven Number 6, in the Afterlife program.

Although there was no wind, a thick mist constantly shifted from place to place. Soft neon-like signs shone in shades of pleasant yellow and pink. The shapes of buildings stood out in the mist, rows and rows of low-rise structures interspersed with courtyards, columned temples, and gothic spires topped with gold and silver. Hugging the winding, narrow streets were small dwellings reminiscent of an Aegean village. White, gold and silver were the dominant colours everywhere, while granite seemed to be a favoured building material.

The streets were full of people, most (but not all) dressed in long white robes or toga style outfits. They moved about peacefully, alone or in small groups, talking happily. Groups chanted in the courtyards of churches and the many treed plazas that dotted the place. Here and there the quiet lull of conversation blended with rhythmic, melodious sounds: hosanna, revival, classical choir, Christian rock, gospel … It could be adapted according to taste depending on how a person focused their listening. *Here* was a quiet liturgy, *there* were the sounds of a revival meeting.

The beauty seemed to go on as far as the eye could see. It was everything a person might imagine Heaven to be. All of it caused euphoria to swell up inside. It was perfectly designed—no hurt, no pain, only a sense of wellbeing prevailed. It was everything one hoped it would be: Paradise, the Afterlife, just as advertised.

The application that had created this wonder was extensive and multifaceted; one choice would lead to a dozen others so every person's experience could be custom-made.

When applying for a personal avatar, and entry to this virtual world, thorough screening was required in order to ensure each person made the appropriate choices to suit their needs. Abundant questions were asked pleasantly and politely until finally each applicant was allowed to choose their avatar and one online reality. Only one avatar and one online reality were allotted per person.

Those who chose Afterlife could expect a reality constructed along religious ideals, whether Biblical or other. Those who chose Otherlife had a variety of options that did not include a deity, including 'new age' beliefs, and even a corporal existence that would appeal to atheists or agnostics.

Before the system became refined, people used to choose whatever avatars they wanted, even animals and cartoon-like characters. However, after the Org streamlined its management of the Afterlife and Otherlife databases, applicants could only choose personas taht fit with the logic of the program. This made animals and cartoon characters inappropriate in Afterlife programs. Further, some options, such as a popular fire-engine-red mist, were banned from Christian Heaven, though allowed to remain in other programs. In Christian heaven it was regarded as a sign of the Antichrist, whereas in some Asian faiths, it was considered good luck.

Because each life was a program, and collectively the system was building up a database for eternity, the integrity of the program had to be maintained for the benefit of all participants. It was important to ensure a certain logic to avoid inconsistencies that could lead to erroneous data. For example, if an atheist wound up in a deity-based afterlife, it would corrupt the system, and so on.

For this reason, continuous quality control and restructuring was necessary. As the system grew, so did its management, which was further broken down according the belief systems it managed. For example, in Heaven Number 2, strict Christian doctrine was adhered to, including the Catholic tradition of confession. In Heaven Number 6 the stringent adherence to doctrine was not emphasized.

Today in Heaven Number 6, an assembly was being held. The Archangel Gabriel was speaking about the 'eternal state of grace', and everyone was pretty pumped up about the idea. There had been some agitation about the ever-expanding existence of espresso bars in Heaven Number 6. Many wondered why they were there, and saw them as one concession too far toward recreating offline life; others found them to be a nice perk. A positive outcome of their existence was that it was detracting from a simmering anti-Catholic hostility. In the rather liberal Heaven Number 6, many citizens didn't appreciate the strictness of that version of Christianity and wanted professed Catholics to move to Heavens Number 2 or 3. There was much bickering. But now the espresso bars were a common enemy.

When not denouncing espresso bars, another favorite target was what residents in Heaven Number

6 called 'Christian agnostics'. Sometimes Christian-identifying people with a wide variety of differing beliefs wound up in Heaven Number 6 because it was so liberal that it accepted many versions of Christian spirituality. This term was a contradiction; no real agnostic would be permitted entrance; nevertheless, some versions of Christianity were so 'out there' it was hard to understand why those responsible for programming had let them in.

Today, Gabriel had spoken on this. He let the population of Heaven Number 6 know he understood their concerns, but—just like offline—faith was not a straight line. They had to believe their own version and let others do the same.

"Just look around you!" Gabriel said, spreading his arms wide. "Your faith has brought you here, and it will continue to assure your place next to Him. Follow your path, for that is the true one for you."

The speech had appeased most. They felt good about their shared Heaven once again when it was over.

"Gabriel is such a wonderful speaker, isn't he, Reverend Lee?" asked one woman, Betty-Anne, of the local reverend.

"Yes, Betty-Anne, he is a good speaker and he has clearly demonstrated that we are on the right path. We have entered a state of grace here in Heaven Number 6," said Reverend Lee. "However, the espresso bars are new temptations and we must resist. As Gabriel says, we are the faithful among the faithful, and our merit comes in our ability to reach the highest expression of faith."

"You say it so well," responded Betty-Anne with a certain amount of artificial sweetness, feeling as uncomfortable with this one on one meeting as she did in her 3D life. Just like there, in Heaven Number 6, sometimes social interaction could be heavy and pitted with the possibility of error; in fact, in many ways it was worse. Offline, while at work waitressing, there were so many types of people she met that she could often forgot her inner shyness and just enjoyed making small talk. But here, things could get more intense.

She had chosen Heaven Number 6 because of her Christian beliefs. She wanted to remain a child of God in her avatar form and had come to believe that her soul was tied to her avatar. But she was having second thoughts. Before joining Heaven Number 6, weekends in her personal life had included revival meetings, Sunday prayers sessions and overzealous religious fervor. This had seemed a gentler version of Heaven … and yet for some reason she kept seeking out the over-religious, who would remain her influences for eternity. *Why do I keep doing that,* she moaned to herself?

Now, here she was in conversation with the good reverend. A people pleaser, Betty-Anne always tried to say the right thing, but with Reverend Lee it was not easy to stay in character as a pious, sweet woman. Once more she wondered why she had chosen this avatar, when deep inside she wanted to be a freer person. Then she wondered if Reverend Lee was actually a reverend offline and doubted it very much; after all, she was Suzanne, church-going waitress and single mother of three.

"I promised Sue-Anne I'd help her with a new 'praise the Lord song," Betty-Anne said. "I think it's going to be our best yet."

"That's wonderful," the reverend told her. "It's good that someone is upholding good, Christian values in Heaven Number 6. I'm going to speak directly with Gabriel about the espresso bars when he comes to give his next message," said Reverend Lee. "I can't believe the proliferation of these dens of sin."

Inside, Betty-Anne rolled her eyes, "Of course, that's extremely important," said Betty-Anne. "We can't allow this to get out of hand—we've all experienced the dangers."

"We'll meet later, after the assembly, Betty-Anne. May God be with you," said the reverend. Then he left.

Unknown to them both, the conversation was monitored and recorded, the data collected and fed into a databank. Betty-Anne and the reverend were flagged with metadata indicating that they were proving to be reliable characters, true to their avatars, in Heaven Number 6 and positive elements for the stability of the program.

CHAPTER 4

Audrey was one of many citizens whose classification entitled her to have a talker. Her offline status was *'unemployable with various disorders, physical restrictions, or challenges'*.

What this meant was that she had been diagnosed with focus attention disorder as well as physical restrictions—mostly because of her weight, which gave her a further classification of *'mobility challenged'*. Her legs had been officially designated unable to carry her weight without assistance.

She was issued a specialty Org-mandated walker, and given the use of a communal mobile unit, housed in the underground parking lot of her building. Considered largely a shut-in because of her classification, she was also eligible for a talker. Never one to miss an opportunity, she applied for the talker service and was approved.

Truth be told, Audrey could walk just fine, but she wasn't going to tell anyone that. She liked her perks.

The talker service was becoming more and more important offline, both from the participant perspective and from The Organization's perspective. People were surprised to find that, offline, face to face conversation could be stimulating and even fun; in fact, some were referring to it as a 'lost art'. The sentiment was the same whether participants had an online life or not.

At first, when the talker service was launched, it was generally considered somewhat strange, outdated and even anti-progress by many; however, as the service grew, it became apparent that people liked it very much. It gave participants a means to express themselves without having to put up with the existential questioning emphasized in traditional therapy.

Previous to the talker program, traditional therapy was deemed essential for people's wellbeing, but it was a great burden on the state, and many didn't seem to like it much. The talker service had a different reception; people liked that they provided the possibility of smiles, laughter, and giggles, reflexes that had largely been lost to everyone except the non-tech, challenged, losers who frequented the world of bistros and vintage shops.

From the Org perspective, therapy remained essential for some and it was a requirement to delve into people's personalities to help them develop a strong, durable, well-balanced avatar. But talkers provided a valuable interactive service as well. Their face to face interaction and subsequent reports provided an overview and 'check-up' on vulnerable participants, a screen for potential problems. In fact, the Org now considered talkers an integral part of the offline-online security system.

Dell and others of his age and status had been solicited for talker jobs because the Org was expanding the talker program. An increasing number of people needed or wanted talkers. Some qualified for them and so applied, like Audrey. Others were mandated them because anti-social behaviour had been detected.

This was a win-win situation. The participants were happy about getting a much-needed service, and the Org was getting intel about what was going in offline homes, not to mention an inside view into brewing dissent. After years of antagonistic and war-like behaviour in the world, the Org was intent on maintaining order.

Audrey opened up her mini-fridge and pulled out the left-over Indian food she'd had delivered the night before. The sun was going down and there was an orange hue coating the walls of her small studio apartment on the third floor of her building. In this building, the whole second and third floors were dedicated to those in similar circumstances as her own.

While Audrey's various disorders and challenges looked significant on paper, she actually felt fit as a fiddle. She didn't mind her Org classification, though. It actually provided her with a great deal of flexibility in her life. Despite her weight, her mobility was not reduced, and so she only used the walker when she was in situations where she might be facially identified by the ever-present CCTV cameras that seemed to be everywhere, recording everyone, and feeding into the giant database that was the sum total of human experience.

In fact, she was really not overweight anymore, though she carried an extra ten pounds or so. She had managed to lose all the weight long ago; but, not wanting to lose the privileges of being considered mobility challenged, she used a weight enhancing app to appear heavier than she was whenever she was reassessed.

She loved her classification and took pains to maintain it, as the chances of being reclassified as 'challenged' if she were ever to give it up were minimal. She needed the classification to keep her apartment, the allowance that came with it to keep herself alive, and the stability of both to buy her time to further some of her projects. Many of her acquaintances were in similar situations and, like her, felt a certain pride in being classified as 'challenged'.

It was, in many ways, the best of all worlds and, as she often put it to her friends, the word 'challenged' had a nice ring to it. She figured that as long as the pop-ups remained relatively constant on her computer (in terms of ads, ops, etc.), she was safe and not likely to be discovered—so what did she have to worry about?

You can fight the system, respect the system, or play the system, she mused. The first was too hard, the second was intellectually problematic, and so the latter was really the only option she felt she had. It wasn't her fault if the system was fucked. The Org, she figured, hated being *wrong*, and this was her ace card. It tended to dissipate any anxieties or worries she had about getting caught and losing her mobility challenged classification.

Online, she had an avatar of her choice, and she had consciously chosen one that didn't stand out too much. She was 'Lyle' in Heaven Number 6; a slim, trim likable man in his fifties, with no outstanding characteristics to draw undue attention from the Org. Offline she tried to live by the same credo—don't draw attention.

She felt comfortable in both skins. When she was assessed by a psychiatrist, as is required when you chose an avatar, she told the doctor she had a father complex, having lost hers at a young age, and so her choosing a man roughly the age of a father figure was consistent with her profile. No algorithm would ever bring it up as suspicious.

She moved her Indian food from the glass container to the pan on the hot-plate next to her mini-fridge, added a little hot sauce for flavour, and poured a glass of red wine from an economy box as she waited for her meal to be ready. She loved this time of the day. The sun was setting and the room was gradually getting darker; the wine was relaxing, and she loved the smell of the spicy food. *What more could I want,* she asked herself?

Audrey was one of the rare people who liked her online and offline lives equally. She loved her studio apartment. It was ideally located; near the river, close to a few green spaces, and with easy access to public transportation. Due to her 'challenged' classification, it was rent controlled, though it was located in a high rent district. The building had been constructed as part of a social integration project and Audrey was lucky enough to have gotten in the door of this initiative. It never really got off the ground after a promising start. As so often happens, public priorities shifted but construction efforts dried up. The program remained—but with no budget to do anything but pay the managers.

On the first floor of her building were shops: a laundromat, a convenience store, a sandwich bar, and a vintage clothing store featuring an espresso machine and a couple of old chairs for clients to sit on as they chatted and drank dark, strong coffee. Audrey felt it somewhat ironic that sitting in those chairs with a coffee actually felt more like Heaven than Heaven Number 6—and it didn't require any programing.

She could often be found at an espresso bar, both online and offline. She was one of those people Org employees, such as Dell Gabo, would call a 'loser'.

Audrey knew she had to be careful to play victim when she was out and about. The Org had cameras everywhere, and being caught abusing the classification system was a punishable offense. But Audrey knew how to fool the cameras. Not only was she aware of their angle, focus and parameters, but she was also able to connect with them from her mobile and manipulate them so it seemed she was doing what she was expected to be doing.

Audrey liked to have a strong sense of control over her environment and her ability to manipulate the cameras gave her a sense of comfort—even superiority. Unlike many, she controlled her own destiny, at least for the most part. Of course, that didn't mean she didn't have dark days when she suspected that she wondered if she was on the Org's radar. Then she asked herself such things as ... *is that nice-looking man behind the counter going to report me to the Org for being too physically able?* But what could she do? This was the way it was, both online and offline.

She knew she was lucky to understand the ins and outs of things, however, and she felt comfortable in the system. For instance, she knew the system fed off multiple information sources, including visual, written, audio, and even sensual. The more you fed it, the more it gathered information, filtered it, and formulated algorithms to further drive the avatars in Afterlife and Otherlife.

Audrey worked this to her advantage. She knew how to feed it offline information that gave the results she wanted online. She often told trustworthy friends, "The more you feed it, the more it gets overloaded—data, data, data, don't we love data!" She knew that intuition was out the window when it came to Org initiatives. Everything had to be backed up by data.

Luckily, Audrey was a computer nerd. Her deceased father had showed her the ropes, teaching her to code, create programs, troubleshoot and basically navigate the digital and quantum online world. One of his favourite sayings was, "Shit in, shit out."

She had learned a great deal from her father, but she definitely didn't have his respect for authority, or for the system in general. She watched her father work his whole, short life on other people's programs and objectives—never his own. That was not the route she intended to take. Her secret mantra had become, "Shit is good, as long as it is *my* shit," and she was teaching it to a select group of others who she had challenged to use it to create their own realities.

CHAPTER 5

Gomez reached for the towel next to his shower door. Every morning, it was the same routine—coffee, a shower, and two slices of toast.

He looked at himself in the mirror. His eyes definitely looked sunken; the grey beard and stringy grey hair needed a trim. *God, I look like crap,* he thought. He was 66 years old and some mornings he looked more like 80. His thin body had no tone, only wrinkled folds of skin hanging on his bones. *Fat people, or rather the 'weight enhanced', really seem to age better,* he thought to himself. *Their skin doesn't sag so much—I look like I've been left out in the rain and half dried.*

He had always found the words 'weight enhanced' to be a joke, but he was starting to wonder if there was something to that term. *Maybe I should eat more, drink more and fatten myself up,* he thought as he pondered his reflection in the mirror. He was doing the drinking part. But then again, what did it matter what he looked like? He had no one to look good for.

He was alone now. Martha had left him long ago. The loss of their daughter had been too much. It had hit her hard. First she'd started having one too many glasses of wine, then two; and then she started spending long mornings staring out the window with a blank look on her face, or hopping from one thing to another on the net.

He couldn't take it and found it depressed him to see her this way. She said he was further bringing her down. Soon they had switched roles. As she started to recover, he got very depressed. That's when she left.

She still sent him care packages. He supposed she felt a certain responsibility to him … or maybe a marriage was just a habit that was hard to lose. But again, what did it matter? He got all his joy online these days. It was much more comfortable there.

With a vaguely Christian background, Gomez had chosen a Christian afterlife for his avatar. Gomez had always kind of believed in a higher power, and Heaven Number 6 corresponded to teachings from his youth. In Heaven Number 6, he was Max, a young vibrant man who was always in a good humour. He was the exact opposite of who Gomez was in his 3D life.

Gomez found it kind of ironic that, dead and gone to heaven, he was more real, more dynamic, than he had ever been, even if it was only a kind of fantasy. Online, he didn't have to think about the death of his daughter in an unfortunate accident, or the fact that his wife had abandoned him.

Gomez thought back to his childhood, his early days. He had started life reasonably well, in a suburban bungalow with his parents and older sister. He was not the most popular kid in the group, but he was not bullied, either. He hadn't needed to see or meet with a social worker, psychologist, or pedagogical counsellor. His had been a remarkably unremarkable childhood and adolescence. As a matter of fact, until the loss of his daughter—and subsequent departure of his wife—he'd sincerely believed his life was on the right track.

After high school, he'd gone on to technical school and excelled. He'd always worked, and except for one or two small health issues, the only thing that ever kept him awake at night wondering if he had put enough away in his retirement savings plan.

It was only after his daughter died and his wife left that his life went sideways and alcohol and drugs became his only escape. In the beginning it was only a glass of wine for dinner; then it turned into a couple of shots of whisky, more wine and finally the cocaine that a friend turned him onto. And he was off to the races.

Afterlife and Otherlife, as much as he considered them controlling and was philosophically opposed to them, became his salvation. When he was diagnosed with a disorder—an 'addiction challenge'—and put into social adjustment therapy, he was trained on how to choose an Afterlife or Otherlife. He joined Heaven Number 6, as it fit what he had learned as a youth about the Christian faith, embraced this fresh start and became Max, a personality he much preferred to that of Gomez.

Being Max changed his life and revived his badly flagging self-esteem. In Heaven Number 6, Max was soon part of a social group, along with friends Lyle, Walrus and Hector. He spent hours chatting, arguing, conspiring, and talking with them. He knew nothing of them offline, as they knew nothing of him. *What would they think of me if they did,* he often asked himself?

Gomez the man, however, had no real contact with offline humans anymore. His life had become nothing more than ordering in, going down to the common room, and napping. Now that he was over 65, he was not authorized to leave his residence without head protection and a walker, which angered him. The application notice for these things had lain on the table next to his laptop for over three years, but he didn't need them and he saw no reason why he should be required to have and use them.

Jake, his only companion in the common room, said he was crazy and just being stubborn for the sake of it. Like Gomez, Jake didn't need a helmet and walker anymore than Gomez did, but he ordered them and followed the rules, using them when he left the building to go to the bistro, or sit in the park and get fresh air.

However, Jake was non-tech and had no avatar—he couldn't do anything online except essential things, like banking and paying his bills—so as far as Gomez was concerned, his opinion didn't really count. No, Gomez decided, he would tough it out. He wouldn't allow the Org to boss him around. Besides, Max was his escape, and slowly becoming his reality.

He moved over to his table, put two slices of toast in the toaster, poured himself a coffee and sat down to check his mobile. Did he have time to go online and check in with the gang at the espresso bar in Heaven Number 6? Would they be there? Was it worth it? He was receiving his first visit from a talker this morning, so he wanted to be mentally present for it.

What a strange concept, thought Gomez, *paying someone to visit poor souls like me just to chat for an hour or two.* He had been ordered to have a talker, mandated as opposed to requesting for one. Why, he wasn't sure, but loneliness was frowned upon by the Org. It was regarded as a negative to wellbeing, which was unacceptable in a well-organized, modern, caring society. There was even an advertising campaign about it. He could see a huge billboard from his window that said, *"Help Fight Loneliness: Engage."*

CHAPTER 6

Dell had been a talker for almost a year now, and it was far more satisfying than he had imagined. He was surprised at how much he enjoyed it; it was not what he had expected at all.

In the beginning, he had only been looking for a way to escape from himself and his fear about no longer having an avatar, but as he became more and more attached to his participants, he started to be as dependant on the exchanges he had with them as they were on the service he offered.

For the hours he spent chatting, going from one participant to the next, he was able to forget himself, or at least be less aware of his anxiety. It's true, he had lost Kata, but in some ways she hadn't left him. She was still a part of him—but she no longer dominated his thoughts. Dell had a *real* life now, and it didn't revolve around his avatar.

Sometimes, Dell would try to remember what it was like to be her, but he was never sure if he was remembering the way it *really* was, or just the way he felt about it. It was part of his consciousness, but it was fading.

Most of the participants in the talker program were at least a generation older than Dell. There were some who were young though, and a few even younger than him. Audrey, for example, was no more than 27. She qualified for assistance and had the right to a talker twice a week. Her weight designation prevented her from going out on her own, so sometimes he accompanied her. She had access to a mobile unit, but was only allowed to use it to get to what were classified as 'essential services' deemed necessary for her wellbeing, such as mandated therapy.

Dell, like most people, belonged to his own therapy group. Attendance was only mandatory once every two weeks. As more and more people retreated into the perfection of Afterlife and Otherlife, the Org had determined that they were not being appropriately socialized. This not only caused antisocial conduct offline, but was creating problems online, such as avatar rejection and database underdevelopment.

In his weekly check-in meetings with the Org, Dell learned this could be a major crisis in the future if not managed properly. The idea that eternal existence online would somehow eliminate offline existential anxiety was proving false. Offline existence and its anxieties continued to be a problem for many, which was a problem for the Org. They had learned from the past, and the world's history of war, that too much anxiety for too many could threaten society and its cohesion.

As a talker, Dell started to really feel like he was making a difference. He found his sessions interesting and more stimulating than he ever imagined. His participants were interesting, clever people. They discussed every topic under the sun and he even found himself joking with them, something he would never do in open or public settings. Of course, he had to ensure that joking remained light and didn't degrade into a sarcasm. Sarcasm, he had learned in his training, masked deeper feelings of frustration and maladjustment, and it was not to be encouraged.

Dell hadn't had a lot of experience with sarcasm in his life. It had always been considered a form of bullying, ever since he was in grade school, and people were reprimanded for being using sarcasm to degrade others. He knew from history classes that sarcasm was once considered a form of entertainment in comedic rituals, and that it had also been used to attack social institutions people did not approve of. Today, it was considered unnecessary and counterproductive.

As a talker, it was part of his job to look out for counterproductive attitudes. He had to admit, they weren't easy to recognize; speaking face to face was new to him and he still had trouble putting tone and facial expressions together. Sarcasm could be a lot like joking in that way.

Dell made his way up the stairs toward his next client's apartment. Mr. Gomez lived on the fourth floor and, since the elevator was slow during meal times, Dell took the stairs. He considered the hike to be the perfect climb—yet another perk of being a talker. He was doing more walking (and climbing) than ever before in his life, and was beginning to enjoy it a great deal. He had never imagined how enjoyable walking was, or entertained the idea of just going for a walk for pleasure.

Reaching the fourth floor, he turned right and was confronted almost immediately by a glass door that required a push code to open it. He could see a receptionist behind a desk and so he knocked on the glass to get her attention. She ignored him and continued to look at her screen. He knocked again, a little harder. She finally looked at him, then returned to the screen again. Dell yelled through the glass, "I'm here to see Mr. Gomez. I'm a talker and I've been sent by the Org to talk with him."

A button was pressed and the glass doors swung open, "Down the hall on your right, room 401A. Next time take the elevator. The stairs are for emergency only."

"Okay, thanks."

While Dell was making his way to Gomez's apartment, Gomez was laid back in Heaven Number 6. He had decided he had time for a quick incarnation as Max before the talker arrived.

He liked being Max far more than he liked being Gomez. As Max, he was a young, good looking and free to come and go as he pleased. Also, with some techniques he'd learned from Lyle, he could even move from Heaven Number 6 to other program realities if he wanted to: Fantasy, deep conviction, or social ideal utopias—they were all there. It really was the best of all worlds. All he'd had to do was choose his avatar, persona history, and attributes and he could be part of it.

Gomez remembered his first entry as Max into Afterlife. He entered to see Gabriel the Archangel meeting with a group of Afterlifers wearing white togas and long gowns. Gabriel spoke of their long trials in life, their sacrifices, their unwavering faith, and their merited recompense. He assured them that God would have very much liked to have been there personally, but was nevertheless with each and every one of them. He said God felt their presence, and he was sure that they all felt His. It was just like he had imagined as a kid.

"Mr. Gomez? Mr. Gomez?"

"What?" Gomez took off the goggles, turned his head and noticed a young man standing in the doorway.

"Are you Mr. Gomez?"

"That's me—are you the talker?"

"Yeah, Dell Gabo."

"Come in, come in. Sorry for the mess. Would you like some tea? I've just made some."

"No thanks," Dell said.

"Sit down, please—I'll be with you in a sec."

Dell sat in an old easy chair covered by what looked like a bed cover. *It's comfortable enough*, he thought. He hated sitting on hard plastic or wooden kitchen chairs; there was no way to stretch out or lean back, which was not at all conducive to listening and talking.

"Pardon me, but am I in your spot Mr. Gomez?" he asked politely when Gomez returned.

"Don't you worry about that; I have no real spot. I move around depending on what I'm doing. I drink, nap, watch television, daydream, or go online—I lead an exciting life."

Dell thought he recognized sarcasm, but it was too early to tell. Maybe it was just a nervous joke. Sometimes participants were nervous during their first encounters and blurted out things that had no real significance. However, he made a mental note to check the definitions around sarcastic behaviour.

The room was small, but cozy. Gomez had a substantive collection of old books, pictures, and paintings. Dell noted the large window, small table, couch and comfortable chairs. He also noticed the console through which Gomez accessed his avatar, Max.

"So, you are a talker?"

"Yes, Mr. Gomez, I'm a talker," answered Dell. "We are sometimes referred to as conversationalists, but 'talker' is good for me." He added, "You have a nice place here, Mr. Gomez."

Gomez didn't respond, he simply looked at Dell and sipped his tea.

"Do you get out much, Mr. Gomez?" asked Dell.

"I go down to the common room on the first floor. I've got no real reason to go out. What would I do? Where would I go? I'm not equipped to go out, really. I'm supposed to have a walker and protection gear. As you know, if you are over 65 you need to get authorization to walk outside without head gear and a walker. But I don't need them, so I don't have them."

"It's a question of safety, Mr. Gomez," Dell said as if he was reading it from the manual. "You can't be too careful. Safety is really important. Someone fell and broke a hip last week—apparently it would have been easily preventable if they were wearing proper protective gear."

Dell wasn't sure that was true, but it was recommended to cite a real accident to ensure the message was received. According to the literature, it was important that the idea of 'better safe than sorry' be imbedded in the synaptic pathways of all participants.

Gomez just nodded. He didn't want to show lack of interest, or give the impression that he could care less, though that was how he felt. He knew he had to be careful how he acted with this talker or word might get back to the Org and he could easily lose his authorizations. *I need to get to know this kid first and figure out what can be said and not said,* he thought.

In the meantime, he decided to make an effort to be nice—at least until he knew who he was dealing with. The kid could have him declared inept in a number of ways if he wasn't careful. He could have him declared antagonistic, which would lead to all kinds of problems for him. He knew this because, as Max, he was learning the ropes in his conversations with Lyle in Heaven Number 6.

"Perhaps we can start by you telling me about yourself … your likes, dislikes, or favourite activities," Dell began. "I guess you've had some pretty noteworthy experiences offline, haven't you? I know it was a lot harder before we had avatars and a chance to choose how we want to live. Personally, I've never known a time when we *couldn't* choose and were stuck with whatever offline life we wound up in. So, Mr. Gomez, what were the most noteworthy events of your offline life?"

'Noteworthy' was the adjective talkers were required to use, rather than 'good' or 'bad', when speaking about the participants' pasts. It was seen as putting a more positive light on things. According to the literature Dell had studied, everyone wanted to be 'noteworthy', to have done 'noteworthy' things, and to have participated in 'noteworthy' activities. The older adjective 'meaningful' carried too much weight and promoted anxiety, as it tended to bring up existential questions.

"I've led a pretty average life," Gomez said cautiously. "I made some mistakes, adjusted, and now one day leads to another."

Gomez had no intention in delving into his past. It would inevitably lead to discussing the loss of his daughter, and the pain of his wife leaving, as well as a host of other issues. He had no desire to do that. He hadn't chosen a talker; he had been *mandated* one. He would do as he was expected to, and be polite, and no more.

He put on a friendly face. "What about you Dell? How do you like being a talker? When I was your age there was no such thing, unless 'social worker' and 'talker' are kind of the same."

"It's quite different," Dell said with a disarming smile. "Talkers provide human contact, face to face, but we don't deal with specific social or psychological problems. We just have conversations with people the way friends used to do. I can propose things to discuss, or you can—it's just for enjoyment, no analysis or evaluation. And to answer your question, I enjoy being a talker. I get to meet and converse with a lot of people. It's very rewarding."

"That's an interesting word," said Gomez. "I'm never sure what people mean by 'rewarding'. Do they mean *satisfying*, or are they saying they receive something in return, and that they benefit somehow?"

The conversation was starting to become a little tense. Dell noticed hostility in Mr. Gomez's voice. Dell had to try to lighten things up a little and get the conversation back on track. There should be nothing too heavy or threatening the first time a talker spoke to someone.

"Mr. Gomez, you seem to be doing really well here. This is a great little apartment, with a lovely view of the outside. It's a good location—very secure," Dell said.

"I'm getting by," Gomez responded. "I'm not complaining, although I could stand fewer restrictions and less control," Gomez said with a smile and faint laugh. "I never could understand why I need to sign in and out when I leave the building. In the old days, you only had to do that when you were in a hospital ward."

"I suppose it's so they can check to make sure you're alright," Dell said optimistically.

"You think?" asked Gomez. "The person at reception never even looks me in the face when I go past."

"They don't need to, Mr. Gomez. The facial recognition does it for them."

"You're right Dell. There is no need—so then why do I need to sign in and out?"

Dell was stumped. Gomez was right; there wasn't any need for signing in and out since cameras followed everyone everywhere. Gomez had a point.

"I can see your point, Mr. Gomez," Dell said. "Maybe I can check that out for you."

Dell tried to be as neutral as possible. In the first week of talker training, they learned about basic brain structures and how they related to conversationalist techniques. He remembered the teacher saying, "We can orient the synaptic development, neurotransmitter stimulation and axon strengthening through reinforcing the good and positive thoughts—cognitive development, popularly known as cognitive behaviour therapy, or CBT." Keeping an even keel in directing the conversation on a positive slope was repeated again and again.

Dell had only been a talker for less than a year, but he had witnessed the disorders and adjustment difficulties caused by an unhealthy brain, and its influence on the mind, even though he didn't quite understand the neurological theory behind it.

"What did you used to do, Mr. Gomez?"

"I was a painter."

"An artist?"

"No, I painted walls, outside, inside of buildings—like these." Gomez pointed around the room without expression.

"That's great. You improved the lives of people, making their environment brighter and fresher. That must have been gratifying."

"I was doing a job for pay," Gomez responded drily. "Though I didn't mind it. However, it got less 'gratifying', so to speak ... so and I replaced it with drugs and alcohol."

Trying to be upbeat, Dell said, "Did you have a vehicle of your own in your working days?"

"Yes, I lost it in the divorce, though. Then I started using public transport—until I reached the age when I had to use a walker. Ever try to use a walker on public transportation?"

"No, but public transportation is adapted to walkers and other aids," Dell said, repeating what he had memorized.

"That's what they say, but in my opinion transport was designed by people who have never used it."

Mr. Gomez obviously had some attitude issues, and Dell was wondering how to steer this conversation to more amiable ground. Dell was aware that many of Gomez's generation had distorted memories about the past. They often remembered it as brighter than it actually was: The music was better, the climate nicer, the food tastier and even the sun was brighter—or at least so they thought. As Dell's trainer said, their minds erase the dangers, the insults, the conflicts, and the opposing ideas. Dell's job was to get them to see how things had improved.

"Listen, Mr. Gomez. Today is about simply getting acquainted, and I am very pleased to meet you. I will be back on Thursday for another talk, a longer one. If you want, I can bring you a walker so we can go out."

"Don't bother with the walker."

Dell said nothing. This could be a problem. He would be in breach of ethics if he knowingly walked with someone over 65, who had no authorization to go out without protective equipment.

"Have you ever tried a mobile transport device, Mr. Gomez?" he asked.

"No, not really my style—I suffer, according to some, from an excess of pride."

"It can be fun and, as your talker, I am entitled to use one as well. Then we'd each have one—or maybe we could get a double passenger one. Anyway, maybe that's more to your liking. We can talk it over next week and go from there."

"No problem—sounds good, Dell," Gomez said pleasantly, suddenly realizing that he may have exposed too much of his real personality. Lyle had warned him not to be too negative. He'd said, "Never say anything you don't want repeated or examined by someone, somewhere."

This was good advice, but now he was forgetting it. He tried to cover, saying graciously, "I enjoyed our conversation, Dell. I hope you don't get the impression that I don't appreciate this service. I look forward to our next meeting—and the mobile transport device sounds like a good idea."

CHAPTER 7

Audrey put on her visualization goggles, sat down at her console, took a sip of coffee, a bite of a cookie, leaned back and became Lyle.

In Heaven Number 6, on a long winding street, a dimly lit yellow sign flashed: *Espresso Bar.* Below the sign were tables on an outdoor patio. There were columns at the rear, and more tables behind them. Most of the tables were occupied by people wearing the white robes and togas that were standard in Christian themed afterlives.

The conversation in the place was animated, and quiet laughter permeated the atmosphere. The sign above the bar read, "Silence is Golden," but it seemed not to apply in a strict sense. While the directive in Heaven Number 6 was 'animated blissfulness and respect', the espresso bar ambience, and the quarter in general, was known for being somewhat 'avant-garde'.

Audrey and her small group of friends met several times a day in Heaven Number 6. It was an ideal place to meet; less conspicuous than many online sites.

Lyle had chosen Number 6 for a variety of reasons. The open interpretation of scripture made it ideal for free discussion without too much scrutiny and there were no fundamentalists; they mostly congregated in Heaven Number 3, where there was a heavy accent on the Old Testament.

In Number 6 you only needed a superficial knowledge of the Bible to get along. Everyone accepted that there was a God, Jesus, some archangels and the general cast of Biblical characters; however, no one expected them to show up except for special events. Obedience and faith were not emphasized as much as in other Heavens, where some true believers were looking for an authentic afterlife experience.

For Audrey and her avatar Lyle, Heaven Number 6 was ideal. Here, she felt free to explore ideas and engage with others.

Audrey took off her goggles when she heard Dell enter her apartment. Dell had been coming for two months on a weekly basis now, and she was enjoying the company very much. In order to ensure she was entitled to keep the service, she was now pretending to take medication for her focus attention disorder. As long as she played the game, she got to keep Dell's services.

"Dell, how are you?" she asked when he walked in.

"I'm good, Audrey. How are you?"

"Great. I was just visiting a few people in my afterlife. I have an avatar named Lyle. How about you Dell? Do you have an avatar?"

"As you know, Audrey, it's against policy to divulge my personal details to you," Dell said with a smile.

Dell felt a pang of unease as he thought about his former life as avatar, Kata. He still had no idea what had happened to her.

Instead of an afterlife, Dell had chosen an otherlife for Kata. She had been part of a new age site, an offshoot of Eastern philosophy, trying to reach universal consciousness and become one with all nature at the molecular level. However, while it sounded ideal when he signed up for it, it turned out to be just plain, hard work. He would finish each session exhausted.

However, Kata had a great rapport with a small group of others who routinely camped alongside a river in the mountains. The meditating was a little much sometimes, but there were lots of extras: Full moons, nature, rising suns, and vivid colours. It certainly was wonderful to spend time there. But being a talker was easier and often more rewarding than meditating 24/7. If and when he got Kata back, he thought he might try to find a site with a little less personal development.

"I thought we could continue our last discussion. I think we were discussing access to green spaces …" Dell began.

TALKER

"Dell, if you don't mind, I would prefer to change the subject a little, to talk about everyday things, fun things … you know, favourite music, food, games. Serious, serious, serious; let's take a break from 'serious'. Let's go for a coffee in the shop below and relax. You're allowed to do that, aren't you?"

"I don't see a problem, Audrey—it's seems to be within the rules, as long as you have your walker with you."

"Great! I'll get my walker and we'll go. I don't need it, but why ruffle weathers if it's not necessary?"

"Agreed, Audrey."

"It's easier to accept the rules and adjust than try to buck them, right Dell? You need to know how the system works, and what the upside and the downside of actions are," said Audrey.

Dell wasn't sure what she meant, so he said, "If you say so, Audrey."

They headed down the elevator to the ground floor. Dell followed Audrey as she led him into the vintage clothing shop.

"Wow, I've never been in a place like this before," said Dell, looking really excited. "They even have a coffee machine and nice chairs to sit in! Look at the bookcase—it's full of books! I don't think I've seen so many books in one place."

"You're kidding me!" said Audrey. "There can't be more than a couple of hundred!"

"I have a participant who has books, but he has maybe a dozen at the most."

Audrey shook her head, as if to say, 'you poor thing'. Then she said, "So Dell, why don't you get us a couple of espresso longs and ask them to put them on my tab."

"I think I'll just have a regular coffee with milk and sugar if you don't mind," Dell said.

"I *do* mind, Dell! Get an espresso long—no milk, no sugar. You've got to start enjoying real coffee."

Dell brought back the espressos and sat down opposite Audrey in an easy chair. He took a sip of the espresso. "Wow, it's not bad," he said. "I didn't think I would like it."

Audrey looked up at a camera above their heads. A light was flashing above it. She said, "Dell, how about moving your chair about two feet to the left?" If he was surprised at the request, he didn't show it. He moved his chair until she said, "That's it—that should be good."

After that, Audrey and Dell sat in silence sipping their espressos, Audrey watching the people pass outside the window while Dell thumbed excitedly through books.

"You know, Dell, you can borrow one of those books if you want. Have you ever read a book?"

"Not a paper one," he said. "Nothing with a cover and real pages."

Audrey laughed. She liked Dell. He was easygoing for an Org worker.

"Well, enjoy yourself then," she said. "I don't really feel like talking today."

CHAPTER 8

Dell sat down at the end of the table in the conference room at the Org head office. At the far end of the table sat Ms. Smith, along with Mr. Sanchez, the motivation manager and Ms. Singh, head of human resources. There was no sign of Mr. Wang or Mr. Fortin, who Dell dealt with normally.

"We'd like to discuss your work with us—your role as a talker," Ms. Smith began.

While he reported weekly to the Org about his talker activities, this was the first time Dell had been in an official meeting with the administration. Talkers generally reported to supervisors via teleconference.

Ms. Smith was once again in control, even if the two others *were* her superiors. It was clear that Ms. Smith carried a lot of weight and was as intimidating to them as she was to him. She had that 'don't interrupt me when I'm talking' look about her.

"Is everything okay?" asked Dell with poorly hidden apprehension in his voice.

"Yes, fine. No problem," said Ms. Smith. "We just want to ask you a few questions about one of your participants, and maybe get your feedback. Mr. Gomez has come to our attention," she said sharply, getting straight to the point.

"Mr. Gomez? Why?" asked Dell.

"Have you noticed anything unusual in your sessions with him?" she persisted.

Dell frowned. "I don't know that I've noticed anything out of the ordinary," he said. "He sometimes has problems seeing some of the benefits of the programs the Org has provided for him, but other than that, it's going well. We mostly discuss personal experiences from his past, like former jobs and problems with addiction. He never mentions the death of his daughter."

"Do you try to talk about his daughter's death, or why his wife left?" asked Ms. Smith. "Maybe he needs to talk about it."

Dell felt he had to be delicate in how he worded his response. He said, "It's possible, Ms. Smith, but my understanding is that I am not to play therapist with my participants, so I would never push him on that matter."

Ms. Smith looked at Dell as if he had misunderstood her. "Records show it was a freak accident. She was hit by a delivery drone at their own front door. It caused quite a stir. That was before the *'Drone in the Vicinity'* app was made obligatory for all devices. As a matter of fact, it was that incident that initiated the present regulation."

"Oh," said Dell.

"Perhaps he's not adjusting properly," said Ms. Smith.

"He just doesn't want to talk about it, and I don't push him," Dell reiterated.

Ms. Smith tried a different approach. She asked, "Does he understand that his health issues stem from his addiction? He's what, 68 years old, and his bio health indicates a man of 75."

"We have not discussed that," said Dell.

"Also, tracking never shows him leaving the building he lives in," added Mr. Sanchez.

"I guess he never does," said Dell. "He told me he is required to use a walker if he leaves, and he doesn't think he needs one, so he doesn't leave."

"Did you explain the importance of safety, and that the rules are in place for his wellbeing?"

"Of course."

"Does he understand that?"

"I guess so. He doesn't say much. I talk more than he does sometimes—I presume that's okay? The literature says that some participants need to talk, but others need to listen. My trainer said, 'listen or talk, but communicate'."

Ms. Smith looked down at her tablet. "He seems to spend most of his time online, especially in Heaven Number 6."

"He has a hand held and a wall screen," said Dell.

"Is it on when you're there?"

"No, but I assume he turns it on when I leave."

"Does he have religious convictions? Do you speak to him about his beliefs? Why did he choose to go to Heaven Number 6?"

"Well," said Dell thoughtfully, "he says he believes in a higher power, and that Number 6 corresponds to his afterlife beliefs."

"Does he talk about or salvation, or universal consciousness … anything like that?"

"Not really, Ms. Smith. He mostly talks about day to day things, such as food, old movies, stuff like that. Once he referred to the good old days, but I corrected him on that."

"Did he argue with you?"

"No, he never argues. He answers my questions, and he's asked me a lot of questions—more than my other participants usually do."

"So, you give him a lot of information?"

"I give information I think I deem important. I thought that was *good*."

"It's neither good nor bad," said Ms. Smith. "It's whether or not it's appropriate for the situation."

"I'm following the guideline," Dell said, feeling a little defensive.

"Does he have any unusual habits, does he make strange comments?"

"He's pretty regular, Ms. Smith."

"What do you mean by 'regular', Dell?"

"I mean, he lives a normal life—nothing exceptional. Other than maybe a dozen or so books and a few appliances, he doesn't own much or seem exceptional in any way."

"Books? Who needs to read paper books these days when all information is online? You don't find that strange, Mr. Gabo? What kind of books does he have?"

"I have no idea, I never really looked," said Dell.

He looked at Ms. Smith with the respect required of him, but he was feeling really uncomfortable now, and thought this was a subject it was best to stay away from.

"Well, Dell, next time you're there, take a look at those books and get back us," Ms. Smith said. We need to complete our profile on Mr. Gomez."

Dell nodded, but he didn't want to do it.

"That will be all, Mr. Gabo," said Ms. Smith.

As Dell walked out of the conference room and down the long hall he wondered, *why the interest in Mr. Gomez?* Every week briefed his superior on all his participants, and Mr. Gomez seemed to be the least problematic. What did they know about Mr. Gomez that he didn't? Their interest was both intriguing and a little uncomfortable.

He decided it would be a good idea to watch what he said about Mr. Gomez from now on, to keep his reports simple and just report what was necessary. He liked Mr. Gomez and felt a certain sense of protectiveness towards him.

"How do you think that went, Ms. Smith?" asked Ms. Singh when Dell was gone. "Are we going to keep Mr. Gabo on as a talker? We've gone to a lot of trouble to recruit him and we're finally getting a good look at the offline lives of those troublemakers in Heaven Number 6."

Mr. Sanchez nodded. "And we wiped out his avatar … what was its name?"

"Kata," said Ms. Smith. Then she said, "We knew this would be a long, gradual process. We knew that by erasing his avatar, he would start be more susceptible to the benefits of becoming a talker. It's working, but we need to give it a little more time."

"Okay, then, what's our next step?" asked Mr. Sanchez.

"The next step is that I take on an avatar and join Heaven Number 6 … and then we continue," said Ms. Smith, leaning back and smiling. "I think I'll be Jan. Ms. Singh, if you could set that up for me, I can probably jump right in with the espresso gang."

Ms. Singh nodded.

Ms. Smith continued, "Make me as attractive and likeable as you can. Set it up so I'm particularly attractive to Mr. Gomez's avatar, Max. Check out what his wife looked like when they first met … you know, pictures, interests, hobbies. Set Jan up so he can't *help* but fall for her."

CHAPTER 9

Lyle and Max walked on until the dim yellow lights came increasingly into focus. As they neared their destination, the word 'Espresso' became clearer and clearer. Now they were able to see the people around the tables, and waiters walking to and fro. They could smell of coffee.

How good it smells, thought Max. Lyle said that before espresso bars, you could only smell lilacs and incense in Heaven Number 6.

Max never understood if Lyle liked the smell of lilacs and incense or not—or even if the program had them smelling the same thing. Smell and taste were new sensations in both Otherlife and Afterlife. It was a big improvement and it made everything so much more realistic.

At their favourite espresso bar sat Jan, newly arrived but already one of the regulars. For Lyle, Jan was most definitely not yet part of their little group, but for Max it was different. Max instantly liked Jan, even though they had just met—she was smart and seemed to know her way around. And, while he couldn't quite put his finger on it, there was something about her that seemed familiar.

"Where have you been?" Jan asked without really expecting an answer.

"Exploring the boundaries with Lyle," replied Max.

"Can you order me a double espresso? I'm going to see who's here," said Lyle to Max as he headed off. Max noted that Lyle didn't really acknowledge Jan.

Max sat down next to Jan. She looked so good. She was pretty and blond. Her white toga was just slightly open, revealing part of a breast. He found it hard to understand why Lyle was less taken by her, and why he told Max and the others to be careful what they said around her—at least until Lyle had a chance to check her out.

Two figures sat at a table next to them, deep in conversation and Max and Jan listened in.

"I don't know. It's all good—no pain, no hunger, nothing bad. It's just, well ... I thought there could be more of an *enlightening*. Do you know what I mean? Kind of an explanation for the way things are, and why? I keep thinking there should be more."

The speaker's companion nodded thoughtfully. The speaker continued. "I mean, it's beautiful in a classical kind of way. I just feel like there should be ... I dunno ... kind of a shock and wonder thing, where you suddenly realize, '*hey* ... so *that's* what it's all about!' Do you get what I mean?"

His companion nodded agreement and then said, "Remember the televangelists back in the day? They used to really have a punch. Don't get me wrong, I chose Number 6 because it was advertised as more laid back, but I thought we would get a little more on stuff like good and evil, salvation and so on ... more like I got back in Sunday school."

"Maybe we'd get more of that kind of thing if we hung out with Reverend Lee and that group," the first one said.

"They're a little too far off the deep end," replied his friend. "They should be in Number 3, if you ask me."

Jan listened carefully, though Max was less interested. This was a variation on a subject Max had heard discussed more than once. Usually, Lyle, Max and the rest of the espresso gang pretty much ignored that type of conversation, though lately they're been pretending to care about such conversations because rumours had been circulating that the Org was keeping tabs on the place. Word was that they were worried about active dissent in this online paradise and might be making modifications.

No one wanted that. It was disappointing. If clampdown made its way into Heaven, it would make it pretty much the same as the 3D world.

"If I'd known the Org was going to turn on us, I'd have chosen a reincarnation application instead," Lyle told Max. Avatars could switch programs by applying, but the waiting time was incredible.

"Anything new?" Max asked Jan as she continued to listen to the conversation.

Jan shifted in her seat and gave Max a big smile. They were becoming more and more comfortable together and his admiration for kept growing. She was absolutely flawless, as far as Max was concerned, and they had a great deal in common. They shared an interest in analyzing the ups and downs of history, they had similar religious belief systems, and they both enjoyed commenting on passers-by. Further, Jan always had just the right compliment for Max, which made him feel like a million bucks.

Jan stirred in her seat once more and took a sip of her coffee. "Look, there are some new arrivals," she said, pointing. "It looks like they arrived together. They probably know each other offline."

"They're settling in pretty quick," Max said.

Sometimes people who were already friends offline would decide join a specific Otherlife or Afterlife together. It was easier to fill out the forms and make choices when you chose as a group.

"Maybe joining after a conflict is a good idea," suggested Max, "That way, you're joining in the spirit of reconciliation."

"That's a great thought, Max," agreed Jan. "That keeps things focused, at least for a while. After that, it might create tension. You and I have no idea who each other is offline, and have brought no baggage. I think it's better that way."

"Maybe you're right," said Max. Then, changing the subject, he asked, "By the way, have you heard about the avatar disappearances, Jan?"

"Not a thing, but I haven't really tried to find out. What about you, have you heard anything? I try to keep my ears open and listen, but I'm new here. I don't really know too much about what's going on."

"I've just heard rumours—there's probably nothing to them," Max said, biting his tongue as he remembered what Lyle had said about giving out too much information. It was Lyle who told him about an avatar named Kata disappearing, and he'd promised not to say anything.

He glanced at Jan once again, and quickly forgot to be cautious. Her body was that of a 22-year-old; her skin was, smooth, tight, and soft-looking and her toga was open. *He didn't think he would be able to feel desire in Heaven, but he did.*

CHAPTER 10

Audrey had good feeling about Max and decided to find out who he was offline. It did not take her long to get Gomez's information. She was surprised to find out he was an older man and found it ironic that Gomez and she were separated by a whole generation just as Max and Lyle were—but in reverse. In that sense, both she and Gomez were young and old souls at once.

Audrey and Gomez had both chosen Heaven Number 6 for different reasons. Gomez found self-worth and pride he hadn't felt for years when he was there as Max, while Audrey discovered a certain freedom as a white, middle-aged male. Gomez wanted something better than his offline life, while Audrey was looking for an addition to what was actually already a fairly robust lifestyle.

Together with some others, they had formed a little online group that they called the 'espresso gang'. Offline, they would be considered people on society's borders; misfits and losers. In Heaven Number 6 they were resisters and disturbers who liked their Heaven just the way it was and were opposed to the Org was clamping down to change its character. They knew some people were opposed to the proliferation of espresso bars, and thought these people should leave Heaven Number 6 rather than bringing the Org down on their heads with their whining—after all, didn't they have enough of those rules offline? A person couldn't go anywhere without proper permits, and CCTV monitored literally *everything*.

Further, they felt entitled to 'work' the system. Just as Audrey had long ago figured out what to do to get the most out of the oppressive Org structure by playing up her special classification, the little group's modus operandi was to get the most out of what the Org had to offer, both online and off. To Audrey's way of thinking, if the Org really wanted people to live in a state of 'wellbeing', then they should encourage people to pursue the things that made them happy. Like peanuts. And coffee.

Audrey wanted to meet Gomez, but she was cautious about Max's developing relationship with Jan. Jan was new and the layers of encryption to her online persona made Audrey suspicious. There was something too situationally correct about her and Audrey didn't like it. She felt she had to be careful.

Though Audrey felt the Org's ability to track, hear, and watch its citizens—both online and off—was vastly overrated, overconfidence was the one sin she didn't want to commit. Penalties for breaking Org rules included losing avatar rights, and even old-school punitive measures like isolation therapy, a remnant from the old 'jail' days.

Gomez/Max had a well-established persona, both online and off, which Audrey appreciated. As Max, he was sometimes a little irreverent with respect to the rules, but he never went too far. That's why he was part was part of her plan to improve the quality of life for him, her, and a select group of friends. So far, Max had come through for her.

She left her building and headed down the street towards the dog park. Estaban and Liliane, part of the espresso gang, were sitting on a bench watching their dogs playing in front of them. Her friend Elroy was standing behind the bench, looking out at the lake.

Online, Estaban went by 'Hector' and 'Liliane' by Walrus. Elroy, as gifted in tech as he was, absolutely refused an avatar and instead he went in and out of Afterlife and Otherlife as different personas depending on his whims and the needs of the group. He saw himself as an irreverent anarchist and played it to the fullest. Taking on a permanent avatar was against his principles.

"Nice dogs. I didn't know you guys had dogs," Audrey said as she approached.

"We don't, but we got a gig looking after them. We take them out for a couple of hours each day for a fee.

That's one of the advantages of living near people in a high rent district—they want to have everything, but don't have time to take care of anything but themselves," said Liliane putting her arm around Estaban. The two of them laughed in unison.

"What are their names?" asked Audrey.

"That one is Kipper, and the other is Slug."

"Why Slug?" she asked as she gave Slug a scratch.

"Looks a little like a slug from the back, don't you think?"

"I don't know if I have ever seen a slug," said Audrey

"A slug looks like that dog, but a lot smaller."

Audrey laughed. Then she said, "Well, it's good we are all here, face to face. It's time to get our little project going."

"What about Max? Is he on board?" asked Estaban.

"I think so, but I need a way of seeing him offline. I know where he lives, more or less. I've tracked his mobile. He's Gomez offline. Albert Gomez."

"Where would you meet him?" asked Liliane.

"I don't know, but we both have the same talker."

"That's interesting. Do you think you can meet through your talker?"

"Not yet. He's new for Max ... but I think if I work it right, there is a way. The talker's name is Dell and he has potential, though he's hard to read. He's pretty discreet, but sometimes he seems to forget his role and opens up a little. It's like he tries to go by the book, but the struggle becomes too great and all of a sudden his true personality comes out. He's more of a rebel than he thinks. He's a rebel without a cause. All he needs is a cause."

"A little like us," said Elroy.

"No, Elroy, you are a rebel who doesn't need a cause—you're a natural."

They all laughed and Elroy did a little dance around the bench. "That's my rebel dance."

"By the way," piped in Estaban, "can you still get into the central Org server?"

"No problem, guys. I just have to follow the data. It's gets easier and easier. They've only changed the password and the identification answers—that's not a problem. The facial identification is easy as shit. Thank god IT experts all take the same courses and training. Fuck, they even get the same upgrades!"

"Yeah, because if they were as good as they thought they were, we'd be fucked," said Liliane.

"Listen, you guys. I need to get back and pretend to take my pills for my disorder," said Audrey.

"Okay, Audrey. Long live your disorder and may it prosper," Liliane joked. "By the way—do you still have some worries about Jan?"

"Yeah, I can't place it. She is too cool. Also, so far I haven't been able to track down her offline persona. I'm looking at the challenge as entertainment."

Audrey gave a thumbs up, turned around, and headed back to her apartment. "I'll walk with you," said Elroy. "I have to print out some more 'challenged' cards and I'm going right by your place."

They walked along with Elroy jumping from side to side, while Audrey went more slowly because of the walker. They had known each other for several years, and although they were never a couple, they were very close, like brother and sister. Audrey was thoughtful, premeditated, and meticulous; Elroy was impetuous and high strung. They were perfectly matched, as Audrey never got tired of reminding Elroy.

CHAPTER 11

Ms. Smith was in the conference room the full executive team—Mr. Fortin, Mr. Wang, Ms. Singh and Mr. Sanchez. It was extremely rare that Ms. Smith met with all four together. Mr. Fortin and Mr. Wang were subordinates and generally not included in priority issues planning.

The meeting was in 'the confidential room'. There were no known microphones, cameras, or other detection devices in the confidential room. Of course, this didn't mean you could say whatever you wanted; a certain care always had to be taken. Participants in meetings in the confidential room were *supposed* to leave their devices outside, but how would you know if they didn't? Occasionally security did spot checks to make sure no one was bringing in a recording device— but no one ever checked Ms. Smith.

"Do we have a problem with Mr. Gomez, Ms. Smith?" asked Ms. Singh

"I really don't know. Our talker seems to feel everything is going relatively normally, but Mr. Gomez's attitude leaves something to be desired. However, this is not uncommon in men from his generation. What astounds me is that his online avatar, Max, seems to be a lot more informed and involved than Gomez is offline."

The group pondered this information, and Ms. Smith looked at them to gauge their reactions.

"Gomez is not really forthcoming to our talker. It's strange, though, that he's so knowledgeable. He spends most of his online time with an avatar named Lyle. I've checked Lyle out, and neither he, nor his offline persona of Audrey, are that interesting. They are very average, somewhat dull personas, with routines that are almost identical every, single day."

"Interesting," said Mr. Singh.

"On another note, my avatar of Jan, who we planted specially to make Gomez's avatar of Max talk, is working well. Max is definitely attracted to Jan, to the point of making what I consider inappropriate advances. I wonder if we haven't made Jan a little *too* enticing."

"Remember, we set Jan up to have sex appeal and an open attitude so Max would be attracted to her," interjected Mr. Sanchez. "Strangely, *offline* Mr. Gomez doesn't seem at all like Max in that or any other way."

"Well, as you know, people often take avatars that are opposite in nature to themselves," said Ms. Smith, "or they take on characters they admire but could never be offline. But we're meeting here today because I smell a rat. Max knows more, far more about insurgent activities than Gomez apparently knows. This is making me suspicious."

Mr. Sanchez said, "You know, I don't think our talker is giving us the information he should—or maybe he's just not capable of discerning Mr. Gomez's real character. Something doesn't match. Maybe one of our special agents can pretend to be a talker and replace that Dell Gabo. We need to have full confidence that we're receiving correct information."

"There is a standard procedure for this kind of situation," said Ms. Singh. "If there is a lack of confidence in the talker's ability or commitment, it is recommended that we inform the talker of the issues and then have a discussion with him in order to determine if the problems are serious or not. Unless we can prove his conduct is inappropriate, or there is a conflict of interest, we can't just dump Mr. Gabo without cause."

Ms. Smith clasped her hands in the chapel position, rested her elbows on the table and looked directly at the group. "Let's leave it as is for the moment," she said ponderously.

"I suppose that means Mr. Gabo shouldn't know that you are observing Gomez online as Jan, Ms. Smith?" asked Sanchez.

"That's right," said Ms. Smith.

Ms. Smith had ideas about how to deal with the situation, but she wasn't yet prepared to share them yet. The creation of Jan wasn't her first intervention via avatar, and Heaven Number 6 wasn't the first place in Afterlife she'd infiltrated. She favoured this direct involvement more than most of her colleagues; how else could she get the pulse of things? Her name was Gabriela, so why not go for the gusto—she would become the archangel Gabriel, as well as Jan, in Heaven Number 6!

As both Jan and the archangel Gabriel, she could socialize with the group, check out Max and his friends out and even give them instructions if need be.

CHAPTER 12

Dell arrived early and sat in the same waiting room he had sat in before his initial interview for the talker job. He reflected on how much things had changed. Everything in his life seemed to be different these days. Were they better or worse? That he couldn't say. But he did feel a lot less naïve.

He got up and made his way to the coffee machine at the far end of the room. It was out of both coffee and water. Slightly aggravated, he searched the cupboards for the coffee and filled the machine up.

When the coffee was made, he poured one and sat down again. As he sipped, he began to reflect on the last couple of days. Through Audrey's hints, he suspected Ms. Smith of having taken on the avatar Jan in Heaven Number 6, where he knew Audrey and her friends hung out—but why? Audrey told him the Org was tracking Gomez/Max. What was all the interest in him? How could old Mr. Gomez be so important that Ms. Smith kept quizzing him about him?

His encounters with Gomez and Audrey, both of whom had mentioned their group of friends and acquaintances in Heaven Number 6, had been benign. In fact, Dell was thinking if he ever got Kata back, he might join them there. They seemed like a good-natured, easy-going group. But his intense meetings with Ms. Smith indicated otherwise. She always wanted to know what he had learned about them, and where it all fit in the bigger scheme of something he didn't understand.

Maybe it doesn't *fit,* thought Dell. *Maybe they are all just insignificant, inconsequential personalities, living their lives … and Ms. Smith is barking up the wrong tree.*

Conversely, maybe these interviews he kept being asked to come to were nothing but part of Org processes, procedures, and protocol.

He sighed. One thing for sure was that ever since he'd become a talker, his world had changed, as had his view of the Org. For example, one thing he'd learned from Audrey was that the well-organized, efficient 'state and corporate machines' were not as efficient as he had imagined. Audrey even mentioned that she had the ability to hack the system. Further, he had learned that Audrey and Gomez knew each other online, and that they were part of a group of friends who regularly had coffee together in Afterlife's Heaven Number 6.

Audrey also often poked fun at the Org's surveillance and control systems, both online and off.

Absolute control was not even possible, according to Audrey—yet Ms. Smith and her team seem to obsess over maintaining it. Dell was beginning to realize that the system had no choice but to believe its own set of truths.

Ms. Smith opened her office door and motioned Dell to enter. "How are we today, Mr. Gabo?"

"Fine, Ms. Smith."

"Is everything under control? How are your clients doing? Are they improving, making good use of the assets provided to them?"

"I think so, Ms. Smith. Mr. Gomez is getting out more. He accepts that he must use a walker, and I think he actually finds it useful."

"So he's realizing the benefits?"

"He seems to be. I believe he's beginning to see the light. He's not quite used to wearing the helmet, but I think that's coming. I really believe Mr. Gomez and I are making progress. He seems more relaxed, more content these days. Getting out has done him a lot of good."

Dell paused and looked at Ms. Smith, who seemed more interested in what he was saying than was comfortable for him. He didn't trust her.

He continued his report. "He's also opening up to me more and more," he said. "Nothing of note to report on that side, but I'll let you know as soon as there is."

Dell thought he noticed Ms. Smith's eyes light up and he knew he was on the right track. He had to manage the information he fed them; he had to protect Gomez yet give the Org enough to think they were going to meet their objective, whatever that might be. Dell knew that Ms. Smith and the team wanted to see progress with his 'infiltration' of Gomez's activities, but it had to subtle or he'd give away the game.

"My fear, Mr. Gabo, is that Mr. Gomez is withdrawing into a cynical, critical mode—that was how you assessed him after your first few encounters. As you know, mental wellbeing is as important as physical wellbeing, in fact they go hand in hand. Mr. Gabo, people don't always know what's good for them. They need to fear what needs to be feared, but appreciate what needs to be appreciated. Some need to be shown what they need to believe, and then constantly have it reinforced."

"Do you mean acceptance conditioning, Ms. Smith?"

"We don't use the word 'conditioning', Mr. Gabo—it's called 'positive avoidance outlooking', meaning fear of what needs to be feared. It's genetic, it's who we are. We are trying to get them to adjust their outlook so it matches their biology."

"I understand, Ms. Smith—and I couldn't agree with you more."

"I'm glad that we are on the same page, Mr. Gabo. Continue with your work and keep me informed if anything out of the ordinary comes up."

Dell felt a chill at her words. Audrey had been trying to tell him that the Org was wrong in its approach to things. She had hinted that she and her friends were resisting the Org's iron fist. Now he knew the truth: Audrey was the answer, not Ms. Smith. Audrey was who he needed to team up with, not Ms. Smith and her cohorts. That was it, he would tell her—he wanted in.

CHAPTER 13

Audrey and Gomez left their walkers and protective gear outside the bistro and entered it from the back, through what was an outdoor patio when weather permitted. The back door was slightly jammed, but Audrey managed to pull it open and let Gomez through.

The bistro was narrow and long, with a bar and tables off to one side. Several customers were sitting at the bar, and one table was occupied by three people. None of the three had mobiles—they were all throwbacks to another, non-tech era.

This bistro tended to attract losers and misfits, which was fine with Gomez and Audrey.

They walked, unnoticed, to the table at the back where Liliane, Estaban, and Elroy sat. To the casual observer, what would be observed at the table was two weight enhanced citizens dressed in sweat suits, and long tall Elroy, dark and sporting an afro. All had a pint of beer in front of them.

When they arrived at the table, Audrey said, "I'd like you to meet Gomez. You know him as Max. Gomez, this is Estaban—you know him as Hector—this is Liliane, or Walrus, and this is Elroy, who is strictly offline, but more tech than anyone in the Org."

"Thanks to Audrey," said Elroy with a smile. "I have a mental and attention span challenge, social challenges and am classified as non-tech, so I am not really expected to be capable of going online much, if at all. I think they used to call it 'digitally challenged', or more politely, 'analog'. Audrey says my status is ideal for moving from persona to persona without ever having a fixed avatar."

"Elroy was categorized as an IQ 60 with reduced cognitive abilities," Audrey explained. "As happens, there was a mix-up or something—maybe the psychiatric team was distracted—so they never really got the genius reading I get. Anyway, it's impossible to re-categorize him now. He's under the care of Estaban and Liliane and they get an allowance and tax credit for looking after him."

"How's that?" asked Gomez.

"They applied for it—filled out the forms online and *poof*, it came through—no questions, no interview—nothing. The system working at its best. It could have been the complete opposite."

"You're kidding me."

"No, you can adopt someone. If you wanted to, you could adopt me. It's all done online. In the old days it required an interview, someone actually physically visiting you—a lot of red tape. Now it can be done pretty easily as long as you know how to fill out the documents. If you know or guess the answer the algorithms are looking for, it's easy.

"Maybe you could adopt *me*," smiled Gomez.

"Yeah, although it would be more difficult because of our classifications—you would need to have deeper cognitive problems, and me less of them."

"Don't worry, Gomez. Audrey has the system down pat—she can fix anything," said Elroy with a smile.

"That's not true, Elroy."

Estaban piped in, "Come on, Audrey—you and Elroy are pretty good at dealing with any shit the Org throws at us. As you guys always say, if there is a form to fill out online, anything can be changed."

Audrey ordered a beer for herself and Gomez, then sat down and adopted a more serious tone. "Okay, guys, we have a problem—Jan, our inspirational, well-adjusted new member in the espresso group. She's been getting closer and closer to Max and is becoming involved in our business. This is a problem, because the talker Gomez and I have has insinuated to Gomez that the Org, and a certain Ms. Gabriela Smith, has a keen interest in him … and we suspect Jan is a plant, possibly a spy. There may be others."

There was a silence around the table—just using the word 'Org' brought a sense of dread, tempered with contempt.

Gomez felt he should justify or explain his situation—but he couldn't. He hadn't caused any waves that might draw attention to himself. He had no idea why the Org was interested in him. Okay, his wife left him and his daughter was killed by a drone … but the Org wasn't interested in those kinds of situations. If he had been targeted, why?

Elroy was the first to speak up. "Are they interested in Gomez, in Max, or us as a group?" He asked. "That's the question. Maybe it's *you*, Audrey—maybe they've figured out your hacking abilities. Maybe they're on to you, to me, to *all* of us."

"Anything is possible," said Audrey, hunching her shoulders. "Sometimes the Org gets obsessed with someone who doesn't fit their patterns. They spend all their time classifying and reclassifying things, so if someone doesn't fit in a box they get bent out of shape. In other words, if they can't explain it, they perceive a problem."

"I hope you're right, Audrey," remarked Liliane.

"Oh, I'm right," said Audrey self-assuredly. "If they found you eating your dessert before your main meal it would be a major problem for them. That's why we need to be careful and protect ourselves both online *and* offline. The Org isn't usually organized enough to make any kind of decision. Generally, one hand never knows what the other is doing. But it's always possible that someone a little sharper than most is on to us and sees nonconformity as a threat. As you know, punishment might be having an avatar eliminated, and none of us wants that. I know they have eliminated avatars in the past—even though it is highly illegal without proof of threat."

"Yes, eliminating someone's avatar without proof of threat is considered a capital offense—it's more grievous than eliminating the person themselves," agreed Estaban. "Eliminating someone offline is only eliminating a determined lifespan that would end anyway … but eliminating someone's persona *online* is eliminating someone for eternity."

"Don't worry," responded Elroy, "they can't eliminate you, but they can change your database so that it has little to do with the one you built up. Do you think they won't play with it once your offline life is over? Who do you think manages the avatar you leave behind?"

"You put too much faith in their abilities, Elroy," said Audrey. "If they systematically tried to do that, they would fuck it up. They are an organization, and by definition the more they try to do, the less they get done. They will never be able to manage all the avatars whose human creators are gone, and even if they do develop a program to do that, they wouldn't be able to decide on management criteria."

"They're not as dumb as you think, Audrey," Elroy protested. Then he conceded, "But they are pretty dumb."

"Well, we have a more serious problem," Audrey informed them. "I found out that my talker, Dell, lost his avatar … and then was seemingly randomly offered a talker job. I wonder if it's a coincidence that he just happens to have both Gomez and me as participants."

Gomez was totally stunned, "You can't be serious Audrey—Dell? No avatar? I can't believe it. He seems so average, someone 'sans histoire'. Jesus almighty. You have to really rock the boat to get your avatar revoked."

"Yeah, that's what I thought. But it's true. I've hacked into his history and I found out he had an avatar called Kata in one of those universal consciousness programs in Otherlife. They're pretty popular these days."

Estaban jumped in, "They are? I could never understand the attraction … okay, I could see visiting one for an afternoon—but to choose it as your program for eternity? Boring. You're just a conscious entity linked to the cosmos—no body, no sensual body pleasures—you can have it."

"Yeah," added Liliane. "Where's the pleasure in reaching a state of oneness with the universe? It's like eating a donut, it's all about the anticipation. Once you mow through that thing, there's no sense of contentment."

Gomez joined the conversation. "I spent a good deal of time trying to know things, figure things out—to understand. I can't say it got me very far. Knowing for knowing's sake is a no-way road."

"I agree, you need to stimulate those dopamine transmitters—keep that donut or cheesecake as an objective," laughed Estaban. "Knowing it's there, and knowing that there is another one if you eat it—that's what's important."

"Speaking of objectives," interrupted Audrey. "Let's work out a strategy to help us figure out why the Org has targeted Gomez, and possibly this group. And let's see if we can figure out whether the Org is behind the disappearance of Dell's avatar."

The rest of the group nodded.

"The point here is that his avatar was eliminated just as he was being bombarded with incentives to become a talker. Then it just happened Gomez and I were assigned to him. Remember, Gomez never even applied for a talker—they just sent him a notice telling him he was getting one."

Nobody spoke. Elroy took a sip of beer and leaned back in his chair. All knew that it was definitely time to start pushing back against the thumb of the Org. They were 'conscientious objectors', a term of the past but a fitting one. They couldn't call themselves revolutionaries; what was there to revolutionize? But they were disturbers, ready to disturb the system to regain their freedom and the right to fuck up.

"Dell has advised Gomez and I that Gabriela Smith is a controller, a guardian of the system. I am more and more convinced that Jan is her avatar. We know she has other avatars in other programs, and we know that she has a special interest in Gomez, both offline and online. The question is, why? I'm trying to hack into her profile, but she's tight. She has good encryption, probably quantum. I'm going to need access to a quantum server if we're going to have a chance."

"What's the plan?" asked Elroy. "To decommission Jan?"

"Nope," said Audrey. "Instead, we'll fight offline and eliminate the digital presence of Gabriela Smith. She won't exist, and she won't be able to feed her avatar databases. We'll keep Jan the way she is, interesting, knowledgeable and attractive to Max, but we'll feed her database with what *we* want... and Max, will have a friend for eternity."

"Wow!" said Liliane. "That's wild! You mean Jan will just stay alive as Jan in Heaven Number 6?"

"That's right," said Audrey. "Jan will stay Jan for eternity, as she is, through her present database. And once we have eliminated Gabriela Smith's offline identity, we may be able to access her other avatars. This could give us a lot of control in Afterlife, depending how many avatars she has, and who they are?"

Estaban raised his glass of beer, "Disturbers, let's drink to the right to fuck up!"

"The right to fuck up!" screamed Elroy loud enough that the whole bistro turned to look at the group.

"Okay you guys, listen," said Audrey. "This is how we're going to do it. First, most of the initial work will be done by Elroy and me. Gomez, Liliane and Estaban, your job will consist of keeping Jan in line in the program and building her database in a way that will be useful for us—or at least won't impede us. Elroy and I will try to hack into the Social Services Directional Department at the Org. To eliminate offline Gabriela Smith we must work backwards. We need to get her digitals, her facials, her various address locations, movements, taxes, certificates, and degrees, until we reach her birth certificate and basics. Then we go the other way, eliminating them one by one as quickly as possible."

Elroy looked at Audrey with a little apprehension, "Sounds good," he said, "but it won't be easy without some inside information and help."

"You're right, Elroy. And that's where our talker, Dell, comes in. I'm going to tell him about how the Org eliminated his Kata, and that Ms. Smith was the lead in that. I'm going to offer him the chance to get even—I'll put it out as us helping *him* rather than him helping *us*."

"And you think he'll go for it?" asked Gomez.

"I think he will, Gomez, with your help. You're good at conspiracy theories—here's your chance to let loose with one. Don't go overboard, of course—just drop hints for a while. From what I can see, Dell is changing. I think he's becoming disillusioned with the Org and that he is moving more and more in our direction."

CHAPTER 14

Dell and Audrey sat opposite each other at a table in the used book store below Audrey's apartment. Dell slowly drank his coffee, a dark, bitter espresso. Audrey had been teaching him to enjoy darker and darker coffee. First he had eliminated the cream and the sugar, then he had gone from a mild blend to a dark blend, and finally he began to enjoy what they called 'Italian espresso'—just like Audrey, who sat there smiling with her own cup, leaning back in her chair with her walker next to her.

She had hacked into the cameras which were replaying yesterday this time at Org headquarters so that unwanted observers would not hear the conversation she was going to have with Dell. She figured they had a good 40 minutes to chat without any chance of observation.

"Listen Dell," she began. "I know about Kata and the fact that you lost your online persona, your avatar. I know you no longer have an online presence."

Dell looked at Audrey in surprise ... yet he wasn't all *that* surprised. He knew she was a capable hacker. "How do you know that—and who else knows?" he asked her quietly.

"I have my ways ... and I only told a couple of friends who have similar interests as mine. Don' worry about it. We're not out to threaten you or do you harm. Actually, we want to help you—and help ourselves at the same time."

Dell stared blankly at her. She carried on. "I think you've suspected some of this about me, haven't you?" He nodded, and she asked, "By the way, just out of curiosity, how important was Kata to you? I mean, if you were to make a list of things that are important— how you see yourself, you know, your identity—would she be right up there at the top?"

"What do you mean?"

"I mean, take me for example—I'm Audrey, categorized as weight enhanced and reduced mobility. I'm female, techno, and not that interesting. Online, however, I'm Lyle—slim, trim, midlife male—and as Lyle I get to enjoy some good, old, white male privilege. But Dell, I'm not really Lyle. For me, Lyle is only a tool. I'm Audrey *playing* Lyle."

"I don't know, Audrey. When I had Kata, I certainly was Kata more than Dell—at least I preferred being Kata. To tell you the truth, now that I don't have an online presence, I'm enjoying being Dell more and more and I feel less and less panicky about having lost Kata. Now what bothers me most is a sense that I have been robbed."

"How would you feel if you lost Dell, and kept Kata?"

"You mean if I lost my *offline* identity? I think I'd be shitting bricks, even though it eventually happens to all of us when we die. But then I think that avatars, no matter how you program them, are not real. Kata was not me, though I was Kata. I've had time to think about that a lot lately."

"Don't kid yourself that our avatars live forever, Dell. That's total bullshit, no matter what the Org says. They remain as long as they suit the program. In the future, they will eliminate avatars as soon as they lack memory space. They will *have* to."

"They're not supposed to."

"They weren't supposed to eliminate your avatar either—but they did. They took Kata from you, wiped her clean, and probably someone else is using her for their own purposes."

"How do you know all this stuff?" he said nervously.

"Relax Dell," said Audrey. "I was curious about you. I knew, as a talker, that you were not supposed to reveal your avatar to me, but when I couldn't find you online—and I'm usually pretty good at that—I went further. And that's how I discovered that the Org rescinded her."

"Can Kata be brought back?"

"Not if they eliminated her database. She would have to be reconfigured and given a new setup—do you know what I mean? If that's the case, then she would be different when you got her back, because her database would be different."

"Shit! Why would they do that? It made me feel so lost."

"Dell, you were supposed to feel lost—the Org wanted you to feel that way so you would apply for the talker position and then feed them information about your 'participants', as they like to say."

"Are you saying that this whole thing is a set-up?"

"Exactly—and you're not the first person the Org has targeted this way. They get you going along, doing your job, so they can add to the files they keep on people like me and Gomez. If you're a good little Org employee, they might even give you another avatar so you can observe and gather information online, just as you are doing offline now. That's the way they work—they're constantly looking for converts and, I'm sorry to say, you seemed like a likely candidate."

"What do you mean 'converts'?" asked Dell.

"Believers in the system; you know, 'we're the best, we're right, we're responsible for the wellbeing of all' … all that shit. Why do you think most of their online programs are belief based? They need lots of belief realities to keep people engaged. It stops them from acting out. Haven't you noticed that they create a new program as soon as a new belief pops up? Now they are creating them for deviant behaviour, building places where avatars can act out offline fantasies, crimes and antisocial behaviour. We've gone from behaviour modification therapy to online crime worlds. As they can keep us online, they don't have to deal with people. Their end goal is for our avatars to even live out everyday activities online. If they could solve the eating and sleeping requirements of our 3D bodies, they would keep us there permanently."

"Shit."

"Shit is right—that's why my belief program revolves around espresso coffee and red wine, and is *offline*. I'm marginal, non-productive, and challenged—but I'm playing all the angles, Dell. Think about it."

"I'm thinking, I'm thinking—I think I need another espresso."

"Go ahead … and get me one while you're at it."

Dell slowly went up to the counter and asked for two more espressos. Audrey picked up her mobile and sent Elroy a message asking for Ms. Smith's digitals and facials, through their new encryption. *Should I show them to Dell,* she wondered? *Is it too soon?*

"Your espresso, Audrey," said Dell, handing her a cup.

"Thanks. And Dell? Don't mention what I said to anyone. I don't want you getting into any trouble—after all, I enjoy having you as a talker. Just think it over, and if I can help in any way with Kata, or anything else—I'm here for you!"

Both sat in silence, sipping their espressos. Many things were running through Dell's mind. Was Audrey right? Was he simply being played by the Org? Had they stolen Kata so they could groom him to be a spy? Could Audrey get Kata back without the Org knowing?

He was just getting used to his life as a talker and he enjoyed going from meeting to meeting. He had a set schedule and little pressure ... except from Ms. Smith, but the reasons for that were becoming clear. He wondered if he could he just ignore everything and continue on. But a door had been opened and now he wanted to walk through.

Their time together was over, so Dell said, "Well, Audrey, we'll see each other on Thursday—no problem?"

"No problem. See you Thursday, Dell. We can meet right here if you want."

CHAPTER 15

Elroy was standing near the regular bench in the park where Audrey and the crew often got together offline. He was wearing an official techno-challenged badge around his neck. This gave him the right to sell outings on the lake in the middle of the park.

Although everyone was stuffed into lifejackets, such outings had recently become controversial, as an elderly lady had drowned three years ago when she leaned too far over the edge to retrieve her glasses. Since then, each boat was required to have railings one metre high.

Some malcontents complained that the railings obstructed their view, but the 'safety paramount' mandate of the Org stipulated that the railings must remain on the basis that it was a small price to pay for avoiding an unfortunate accident. Further, Elroy was required to read a disclaimer to patrons before they climbed on board and remind them that they must stay an appropriate distance from those railings while on the watercraft.

Elroy was good at reading people, and by whispering to just the right ones, he was picking up a little cash. Some boats had adjustable railings; for those, he discreetly sold tickets at a premium, promising customers he would keep the railings lower for an unobstructed view. The trick was to keep the lower railing side of the boat turned toward the open water side, out of sight of any inspector or safety-conscious citizen.

Audrey approached the bench and sat down in front of Elroy. "How's it going? Lots of no-railing sails today?"

"No, too many inspectors around," said Elroy. "What about Dell, is he on board?"

"He's inching toward it. I think the loss of his avatar was pretty traumatic for him and he's probably contemplating what he can and should do about it. You know, he's going through the normal 'let it go or get revenge' dilemma."

Elroy nodded his understanding. Then Audrey asked, "Can you get me into the Org on your next check-in?"

"Sure," he said. "What's up?"

"I have to find intel on a 'Gabriela Smith'. She's some sort of a top dog there. We need to get her offline identity and clearance level."

"Is this part of your nefarious plan?" teased Elroy.

"Yup. I figure you can do your 'I'm crazier than shit act' and have a crisis and I'll accompany you as your caring friend. When I leave you with the phycologist, I'm going to look for an unguarded terminal so I can get into their database and get this bitch's identity."

"That could work," said Elroy.

"By the way, Dell's avatar was named Kata, so if you come across any info or traces when you're cruising around online, you know what to do."

"What about the others? What are their roles in this scheme?"

"They don't know the ins and outs yet, but you and I will give them hints next time we're at the espresso bar."

"Sounds good," said Elroy.

"Okay, see you online a little later. Come in as Goodman. I'll be Tulip. We can meet in Otherlife for a change. I like to watch everyone meditating."

Elroy nodded his assent and got back to work.

Audrey grabbed her walker and walked slowly past the cameras that were facing the street. She felt like drinking a good double espresso and relaxing in one of the deep armchairs in the second hand store below her apartment. She was tired and needed to gather her thoughts. Things were moving ahead with her money-making scheme. She just needed Dell onboard, and they'd be off to the races.

On her way back to her building, few people glanced at her; most were absorbed in looking down at their mobiles. *They're probably online,* thought Audrey.

When Audrey was just across the street, though there was no traffic, she waited obediently for the walk sign to flash that it was safe to cross, and a buzzer sound as well. Cameras covered all angles here, and she didn't want to come up on a watch list for disobeying traffic signs. 'Be visible, but invisible' was her motto. *What they expect is what they get,* she thought.

She walked into the vintage shop, went to the espresso machine and made herself a double. Laying back in the easy chair, she once again had the feeling of being in Heaven—relaxed, satisfied and a little exited for the events about to unfold.

It sounds like a plot to a movie, she thought, as she laid back in the chair. She figured her chances of success were less that her chances of failure—but what was the downside of failure? An online ban? Being forbidden to use her mobile transport? Actually the punishment would probably be six months of rehabilitation.

She laughed out loud at the thought.

CHAPTER 16

Audrey brought out a bottle of wine, one she had been saving for a special occasion. The stew had been cooking in the crockpot since 9:00 a.m., and the room was filling up with a sweet, savory smell. Audrey went in and out of her apartment several times just to enjoy the pleasure of the smell as she re-entered. *All the new technologies still don't come close to the real thing*, thought Audrey. *There is a coziness to the smell of a real, home-cooked meal that is impossible to replicate.*

Dell would be arriving soon. In their talking sessions, she had slowly been revealing more and more of her strategy and plan to him, and she had invited him here tonight to do her final pitch. He was slowly coming around; he was smart enough to see the advantages to her scheme, and young enough to take a chance—at least Audrey thought he was.

She had to reveal things carefully, in case she was wrong about him, and so she had taken pains to talk to him about where things were headed under the Org rules, and how they could be better. She also alluded to the role she wanted him to play; now, she just needed him to get on board.

Dell had an important role to play in her plan—actually it was *the* most important role, because her whole plan depended on Dell and his connection to the Org. If he accepted the mission, he would be in a position to make decisions that would affect them all—but he had to be willing to assume that role.

The knock on the door was soft. It repeated two more times; it was definitely Dell. Dell had a characteristic knock, discreet but audible—not like Elroy, who knocked as if he planned to break the door down, or Gomez who knocked continuously until you opened the door.

Her talking sessions with Dell had made Audrey much more aware of people's mannerisms. She hadn't noticed such things before, as she was much more interested in coding, creating algorithms, or hacking. Now, she would observe all manner of little things, like the way a person sipped a coffee, or a beer. Some took a big gulp right off the bat, others sipped once or twice. Her was pleased at how much more she felt engaged in the offline world. She was discovering a whole new type of existence, sometimes subtle, sometimes loud and in your face, but always full of nuances that were unachievable by AI.

Audrey opened the door. "Good evening, Audrey," Dell greeted her.

"Hi, Dell," she said. She ushered him in and sat him down at the table in front of a plate and wine glass.

"A little glass of red to start off, Dell," she said, pouring the wine.

"What a good idea," said Dell with a smile.

He was not here as a talker; tonight he was here as a friend.

He smelled the food, admired the effort Audrey had made on his behalf, and relished the comfort of it all. This was good. It was almost enough to make him forget about Kata and the online life he no longer had. He was finding offline life more and more stimulating.

He smiled at Audrey again and felt a deep sense of belonging, a good feeling of being part of something. He knew she was going to ask him if he wanted to be part of her little group so he decided to beat her to the punch.

"Audrey, before you start trying to convince me about getting on board with your group and your scheme, I just want to let you know that I am in—on board, ready for whatever comes down," he said.

Audrey was surprised. "Wow, Dell, I had my little speech ready to convince you and it looks like I don't need it anymore"

"Were the wine and the meal part of the argument?" laughed Dell.

"Yeah, but now I guess we'll have to enjoy it for the sake of enjoying it."

"I'm for that! So tell me about your friends and your plan. I know Ms. Smith and the Org are part of it, and I've figured out that you probably want me to help as I'm the only one of the group who works at the Org. Am I right?"

Audrey smiled and dished up the food.

"That's right," she said as she loaded up his plate. "We need you. You're our entry into the Org. Plus you have the smarts to carry out your part of the plan."

"Which is?" he asked as he tried the delicious stew Audrey served him.

"First, as talker, you're going to tell Ms. Smith that Gomez seems a little agitated and is presenting with a lot of negative talk—you know how they can't tolerate negative talk. Don't say anything specific, just tell her it's only an impression you're getting at the moment. We need her to want you to investigate further, and to give you access to their surveillance system."

Audrey sat down and tasted her own stew. It was delicious.

"Once you have access," she continued, "Elroy and I will take it from there. What I need is her entry code and her password. That isn't too hard to get if you know where to look. The Org keeps a databank listing all its employees' recent passwords. It's maintained by an administrator, who I happen to know is not the sharpest knife in the drawer. He usually leaves it unencrypted. When you're filing your reports for Ms. Smith, just link to his system. Then you can let us in."

"How do I do that?" asked Dell, between bites.

"You log in as you, and then you send him a script in a text. I'll give it to you. Once he opens your message, I can enter through you. Then I'll crash the system. You'll have to contact Ms. Smith right away and tell her you were in the middle of typing up some pertinent info on Gomez when the failure happened. My guess is that Ms. Smith will be pretty interested in that, and that she won't wait for IT to take care of your problem. She will give you access to her computer so she can see that report."

"How do you know?"

"Experience—people in authority always feel they have the right, even the obligation, to override their own rules. What's the point of making rules if you actually have to follow them?" she mused. "People who make rules make them for others, not for themselves." Audrey laughed as she took another sip of wine.

"What happens next?" Dell asked.

"Well, Max will start getting cold on Jan in Heaven Number 6. He'll be subtle, but he and the others will start to exclude her, which will drive Gabriela Smith crazy. For example, if Jan shows up while Hector, Walrus, Lyle, and Max are talking, they'll suddenly change the subject in a noticeable way. It will happen just enough to make Jan think she's losing her charm.

That will make Ms. Smith worry and she'll start currying favour with you, trying to get more intel on Gomez, and probably me as well."

"Won't she be suspicious that I'm in on it?"

"Why? It's normal for you to meet with me and Gomez. It's your job. Remember, she set you up for that, to spy on us. From her point of view, you're on *her* team, not ours. She still believes that, or you wouldn't still be a talker."

"What a bitch!" said Dell bitterly. "I was really manipulated, wasn't I? When I think about the notices, the performance tests, the interviews and all the rest of the crap they put me through, it just pisses me off. The whole thing was planned from the beginning when they took Kata. Shit! They really played me."

"We've all been played one time or another," Audrey comforted him. You weren't the first and you won't be the last. But now we're going to play Ms. Smith … and if it works you'll be the winner in the end."

"Dell Gabo, super spy. I like it," said Dell as he lifted his glass in a toast. "Here's to our team!"

Dell and Audrey each took another sip of wine.

CHAPTER 17

Audrey and Gomez approached the bistro from different directions, both moving slowly with their walkers, conscious of CCTV cameras when they passed in front of them.

Audrey made sure Gomez knew where all the cameras in the vicinity of his apartment were, as well as in the places they met.

Gomez was the first to enter the bistro. He made his way to the back, to a table near the window facing the alley.

Audrey came in and greeted the bartender. He cheerfully acknowledged her as the regular she was. He knew Audrey and Gomez had the same talker and therapy group, so he waved at Gomez as Audrey made her way to the table where he sat.

"Let's start with a beer and some fries—then we can plan our next moves," said Audrey to Gomez.

"Good, I like your sense of priority," Gomez replied.

The beer came, followed by fries, which they split. As they ate, they noticed the bistro filling up with clients who were coming in for their weekend drinks. It was Friday and the security checks arrived in their accounts on Thursday, so they were all feeling rich today.

"Here's the game, Gomez," Audrey said when the waitress had cleared their plates. "Your job is to get to Jan—actually to get to Gabriela Smith *through* Jan. You need to get her in an awkward position—make a pass at her or compromise her somehow—but be careful not to put anything in her database you don't want. If we manage to separate Ms. Smith from this avatar, then Jan will become a product of what you feed into her database, so go easy. You fine with that?"

"Actually, it sounds like it could be fun—a little online incorrectness is always attractive. Especially in Number 6 where we're allowed to confess and be forgiven."

CHAPTER 18

Lyle placed a chair out on the balcony, and then retrieved two others from well-appointed living room behind him. The group had access to a wonderful apartment in Heaven Number 6 that overlooked a shady, pleasant street, and he had invited Max and Jan to visit with him there. They sat together on the balcony and watched passersby stroll the peaceful boulevards below, in their white robes and togas.

They could just as easily have stood to watch this parade—in their avatar forms there was no physical need to sit; more, it was a social convention. Online or offline, some things don't change.

Chairs were a concession the Org had made for Heaven Number 6, but there were still some who remembered a time when there were none, back in the days when Afterlife had been a very basic program.

Lyle had invited Max and Jan over for a change of pace, something different than the espresso bar where they usually met. They sat out on the balcony, making comfortable small talk, and then Lyle blurted out,

"Jan, why don't you stay here with Max tonight?" Jan looked uncomfortable. Lyle added, "I thought maybe you two would like to be alone."

"Oh," said Jan, flustered. Gazing up at Max, she asked, "Is that okay in a Christian program? Don't you have to tell someone?"

"Of course it's okay," Max said, "but it's best not to let anyone know. Sometimes, Walrus and Hector stay here—you should see what they get up to! From their accounts, it's better than a porno otherlife," he chuckled. Then he added thoughtfully, "I understand they actually *have* a porno otherlife now."

Jan looked surprised. She said, "Don't get me wrong, I like the idea of staying here with you, Max … but I'm a little nervous."

Lyle got up to leave. "Listen, you guys … I'm going out to roam and see what I can see. Mi casa es su casa."

Before Jan could protest, Lyle headed out, drifting down the narrow stairs and out into the street. Max and Jan watched him walk off, until his figure disappeared into the mist and he was indistinguishable from anyone else.

"Nice man, Lyle," said Jan, appearing more and more awkward with the situation.

"Yeah, I like Lyle. If I hadn't have met him here, I'd be spending most of my time chanting and singing, or playing with my rosary."

Max put his hand on Jan's shoulder. Even though not perfected to 100 percent, they could both feel bodily sensations and the warmth of touch.

"That feels good, Max, but please … not too far."

"Relax, Jan. You seem to feel the same way toward me as I do toward to you. Has it all been an act? Or are you really attracted to me?"

Jan felted trapped in her persona; he was right, her database was aligned with her attraction and affection toward Max. Ms. Smith knew differently, but Jan was in a conflict between her online persona and her offline creator's will—driven by Ms. Smith, but designed to please Max.

She shifted her chair to face Max. They were knee to knee. Max began to stroke Jan's knees and then her thighs. The sensation was there, it felt real. Max moved his hands up and inside her thighs.

Conflicted, Jan said, "Not too far, Max … okay, continue … no stop … yes, keep going."

Max stroked the inside of her thighs with one hand and loosened her robe with the others.

"We need to move off the balcony," she whispered, "People will see us if they look up."

Max looked inside the dwelling. The only completely hidden area was at the back, in the corner. They moved off their chairs and toward the back wall. Both their robes fell to the floor, exposing their naked bodies.

Damn! What is going on, Gabriela Smith wondered? She suddenly lost control over Jan—they were disconnected, and it seemed as if she was shut out of the afterlife program entirely. She switched to the avatar of the archangel, Gabriel, but nothing was there either. It seemed impossible, but she was locked out of the site, out of the program and even out of the system!

I don't understand, she thought. She was blocked. *Gabriela Smith, access,* she typed—nothing, only an 'UNAUTHORIZED' sign on the screen. *Maybe I missed a letter in my user name?* She tried again, but it was still the same thing: UNAUTHORIZED. A new sign now popped up on her computer saying it would be shutting down in 5—4 —3 —2 —1 … and the screen was black.

In Afterlife, Jan went on automatic, straight to her default design. Her mandate was to attract and please Max. She dropped to her knees and began to caress his penis, surprising him. He thought it was only ornamental. Certainly, he'd never been used for anything. Nevertheless, Jan's caresses brought sensation to his lower body and his penis began to grow stiff. This was not supposed to happen—or was it? If it was happening, then it was obviously coded to happen.

Jan took his balls in the cup of her two hands and placed her mouth on his penis, moving up and down. *God, I'm going to come—no it's too soon!*

He lifted her head up and they stood. She put her legs around his waist and guided him into her. It was beautiful, she was so light that it was effortless. They both held back their cries as she moved up and down, and the sensation of coming happened to both of them at the same moment.

"Jesus, Jan, that was fantastic," Max said when he'd caught his breath. "I never knew … it's the first time … Well, I never thought it possible. It's amazing! It felt just like the real thing, but there's no sperm—nothing to clean up. Look, we're not even sweating."

Jan said nothing; she was a little stunned from the sudden changeover that occurred when Gabriel Smith was severed from her. Meanwhile, Max was eager to go again. She consented and they tried as many positions as they could, even using the three chairs as props, in as many ways as their imaginations allowed them.

Finally Jan said it would be good to give it a rest. Max agreed and suggested returning to the espresso bar. They left the room, went out into the misty, white, street, and walked hand in hand down the street to the espresso bar, past the roman columned buildings with their silver and gold fringes.

Heaven Number 6 was in the middle of some festive programing. Sounds of gospel and shouts of 'hosanna!' were being generated throughout; the lighting was even whiter and brighter than usual. This happened occasionally, but this time it was even more spectacular than normal, and both Max and Jan couldn't help feeling a rush of excitement and pleasure. It was, to put it mildly, heavenly.

Jan, however, felt strange and confused. She felt like she was Jan, but *not* Jan. Luckily, the feeling wasn't bad; in fact, it was actually quite good. Severed from Gabriela Smith, Jan was changing even as they walked, her database modifying with the experiences she was having, the surroundings, Max, and her attachment to him taking over from the place Ms. Smith used to be. She was losing her anger as well as any pretenses. Niceness and sweetness were now supplanting the insincere programming she had previously contained. She was becoming the Jan she had only pretended to be. Her database was in sync; it was perfect harmony.

Slowly she adjusted to her new self and began to feel more and more comfortable with who she was—Jan, a sweet woman who lived in Heaven Number 6. She smiled at Max and they walked into the espresso bar, holding hands like two young lovers.

Inside, she was greeted by smiling faces, who had been less than friendly for the past few days—and one new face, a woman.

"Welcome back, Jan," said Lyle. "Let me introduce you to Kata. Kata, this is Jan."

"Pleased to meet you," said Kata with a smile.

"Jan, we are extremely happy you have joined our little group," said Lyle. "You and Max will be good for each other."

Max looked at Jan and held her hand as he said, "You and I are meant for each other. We're both attractive, young, and perfectly compatible. Lyle has assured me that we will become more and more in sync over time, from mind to flesh—or at least to the extent Heaven Number 6 will allow." Then he kissed her and said, "Here's to us, for eternity."

Hector slapped Walrus on the arm and said, "Now maybe we can get some alcohol in this espresso bar. What do you think, Lyle?"

"I think Kata is going to be able to help us with that," Lyle said.

"I'm sure things are going to improve," said Walrus.

"Oh yes they will!" said Lyle optimistically. "Okay, people. This is where we will meet online, and now our goal is to create a little bit of Heaven offline. Oh, and by the way … Hector's idea about alcohol in espresso bars is great. Kata, you can you start working on that right away."

"Here's to bars in Heaven!" said Kata.

CHAPTER 19

Ms. Smith closed down her computer, frustrated. It was the last thing she expected, to be shut out of a system that she managed. How did it happen? She wasn't supposed to lose control over Jan. Now Jan would be on her own, following her instincts without direction.

She felt a sudden urge to drop everything, head home, see her daughter and reconnect with her real existence. She had done her duty, fulfilled her responsibilities—now she needed out. *Tomorrow is another day,* she thought.

As soon as she left the office, she was no longer Ms. Smith, but simply a single mother of one. At work, she was the hard-working, hard-nosed Ms. Smith who had to keep the Org running smoothly by keeping system-buckers under control. At home, she was a woman who enjoyed a nice glass of wine and a hug from her daughter.

Whatever happened with Jan online was probably only a small glitch. No doubt it would be dealt through system refreshment before she arrived at work tomorrow. Of course it could be a hack, or an error in Jan's coding; however, she had no doubt the tech team could fix it. In a way, she was glad it had happened as it made her leave her desk early. She was looking forward to some rest and relaxation.

The metro took her to within a block of her condo building and then the elevator took her to the twenty-second floor and her beautiful condo overlooking the park, with the ocean in the distance. Her daughter wasn't there—she had gone to her father's for the night. *Too bad,* thought Gabriela. It would have been fun to pull head over to the park for a fast walk with her and then pick up some treats on the way back. No matter, it was time to pour herself a drink, relax and try not to think about anything office related. There was nothing to be done for the moment.

After an agitated but reasonable sleep, Gabriela got up early the next morning. She made her way to the kitchen, poured herself a coffee from the freshly-brewed pot she had set up the night before, opened her laptop and entered her password—nothing. She re-entered the password, and still had no access. She couldn't get into the Org's system.

Her stress mounted, as did panic she tried to ignore. It hadn't happened for years, this feeling of lack of control over her situation. She was not a person who lost control.

She went into her study and tried connecting through her desktop computer—still nothing. She tried to get into her personal accounts and had no access to them either. She rebooted her computer, but when it prompted her for a password, the one she gave it wouldn't work. Now she was shut off from *everything*. Nothing, nothing, nothing. Fear took her—without access to her personal files, everything in her house that was hooked to her online accounts no longer worked, including her fridge, stove, heating system, water account, and so on. It was unprecedented that these things should suddenly not recognize her. *What in heavenly Christ is going on,* she wondered?

The office, she had to get to the office.

She got dressed, threw on a coat and left her apartment. At the elevator, her key card wouldn't work. Luckily, a neighbour was on his way out.

"Good morning, Gabriela," he said.

"Good morning, John," she replied. She smiled at him, "I'll let you go first. I lost my key card somewhere. I'll have to pick up another at the security desk. Can you buzz me, please? I'm in a bit of a hurry—emergency at the office."

"Don't worry Gabriela, I can let you out. Just buzz me if you have a problem later."

"Thanks, John. I owe you one."

She walked the ten blocks to her office instead of taking the metro. She couldn't take a chance of any more complications. She had to get to the office and deal with the situation.

The walk seemed a lot shorter than it was, as her mind was busy churning about what may have happened the whole way to work.

When she finally arrived at her office building, she hurried up the stairs to the front entrance, big glass doors and massive stories above.

She felt a curious mixture of dread and relief as she approached the security guard at the entrance. She looked him in the eye, as she had done for years, greeted him and expected him to unlock the door. Instead he said, "I'm sorry, but you don't have authorization to enter."

"That's not possible," she replied, shocked. "You know who I am. I'm Gabriela Smith. I've been coming into this building and greeting you for more than ten years, and you've been here for the last five of those. You're Jeb Darby," said Ms. Smith in a menacing tone.

"I'm sorry, but I don't have any record of your code, and no facial either. Nothing comes up on my screen and I can't let you enter."

"Darby, call someone up top and get me the authorization!"

"I don't have clearance for that," said Darby. "And rules are rules. Nobody can enter this building without appropriate identification codes and facials."

"Jeb Darby, I helped to *create* those codes!"

"My instructions are clear. No acknowledgement without an identity code, facial, and description."

Ms. Smith looked up at the monitor and noticed the small light flashing yellow. She knew what it meant. It meant that she was a non-identified facial—that her facial was not in the system. It was an alert that would go to security. She had created the system; yellow for non-identified and red for unauthorized. Just yesterday, she would have been given a report on that very thing.

She knew the procedure; there would be an investigation to find out who she was and why her facial was not in the records. Currently, she was 'code yellow' and non-priority. Code red meant she would be on a security alert watchlist.

She couldn't believe it. The very system she had created was now working against her. She had a long road of red tape to go through to get her classification back—if she was lucky enough to even get it back. It could take months.

She had to do something. Never mind Jan, Gabriel, or any of the other Afterlife or Otherlife personas she maintained; it was *Gabriela Smith* who was up shit creek. She needed to think—time to work out what to do.

She exited the building and headed down the street, avoiding the CCTV cameras as best she could. Panic slowly overtook her as she contemplated the many possible scenarios ahead of her. She knew the system better than most. If she had *really* lost her offline identity, she was screwed. Her job, her accounts, her access to *everything* would be gone. If it was true, she was basically nobody, just another loser—wiped clean. What to do, where to go?

Elroy stood on the corner as Ms. Smith approached.

"Lady, I think you need some help, maybe some answers. Am I right?"

Ms. Smith tried to ignore Elroy and go around him. He was obviously a loser, probably a non-tech and a hustler. As much as the Org tried to keep such people off the streets, they were always around.

"I think, Ms. Smith, Gabriela Smith, that you want to go to this little bistro near here. You'll find the atmosphere pleasant, and you may find some answers to your predicament as well. Here's the address. It's up to you."

She took the slip of paper without saying a word. *What choice do I have,* she thought? On it was the address of a was a bar where non-techs, or 'outsider losers' as she and her colleagues liked to refer to them, hung out. At those places, little effort was made to do facials. She would have a moment to herself to think without being scanned and reported. She didn't need the hassle, and she did need a drink.

The bistro was adjacent to a thrift shop. She entered and sat at a table in the far end, with her back to the wall. The regular patrons looked at her inquisitively. She didn't look like them; her dress, style and demeanor were not part of their world, unless they had to deal with an Org agent or something.

"What can I get you, ma'am?" asked the weight enhanced male behind the bar.

"Scotch, if you have it."

"A little early for that, don't you think? Are you sure you don't want tequila and tomato juice? It's a great breakfast drink."

"Okay, sounds good … but double the tequila."

"Anything else with that? We have pickled eggs."

"No, just the drink, thanks," said Ms. Smith as she sat. This was very early for a drink in Ms. Smith's world, but what else could she do? Thinking made her panic and she needed to stay cool. Alcohol would at least numb her.

When her drink was in her hand, Ms. Smith sat back and sipped it, but the tequila didn't do anything to reduce the desperation she felt. She was going to need more than one.

Her situation kept churning through her mind. The problem was that she knew the system too well, she knew what it meant to lose your online identity, and how difficult it was to get it back. She had practically created the security system herself; the failsafe procedures; the checks and double checks; the multiple encryption. Losing an identity was a practical possibility, the worst of all situations, a theoretical impossibility—and there was no system in place to remedy a theoretical impossibility.

As Ms. Smith continued to contemplate her situation, two people entered and walked towards her table; a tall, male-identified with dark skin wearing a top hat, who she recognized from the street, and a short, slightly weight enhanced female-identified with a walker she obviously didn't need. They greeted the bartender as if they knew him and then walked toward her.

"Ms. Smith, can we join you?" the female-identified asked.

"Who are you? I don't believe I know you," she said in alarm.

"Let's just say we are aware of your present situation, and we are here to explain, and hopefully to help you."

Gabriela instinctively knew they were responsible. "Well, it looks like I don't have a choice," she said.

"You *always* have a choice, Ms. Smith, but you know better than anyone that the wrong choice has consequences," said the woman. "I'm Audrey. You might know me as my avatar, Lyle. This is Elroy and, except for meeting him a few minutes ago, you probably don't know him. He's challenged, he keeps a low profile." At this, Audrey smiled, though Ms. Smith didn't know why.

Audrey continued, "First, Ms. Smith, you have nothing to worry about, you will soon have an identity back—but not the same one. However, you should be able to live with the one you will have. You will still be Gabriela Smith, you will keep your apartment, and your deal with your ex regarding your daughter will remain the same. Basically, your private life will not change. However, things are going to change professionally. Your role at the Org will be very different. You will no longer have as much status and you'll have no decisional power."

Gabriela was shocked, but her face didn't reveal it. She was also angry … who did these people think they were?

Audrey went on, "You can cooperate or not, it won't make much difference—without your identity codes and facials you are pretty much without options. But if you play along, your offline life will carry on without a problem. In fact, it might even be better … less stress and more free time. Here's what's going to happen. Starting today, you will be my and Albert Gomez's talker. You remember Gomez, right? You've been prying into his business for months now."

Gabriela flinched a little. It was starting to make sense who these people were. It was the coffee gang from Heaven Number 6!

As if reading her mind, Audrey said, "Interesting, eh? You always wanted to keep an eye on us, and now you can! Basically, you will be 'Gaby', with Dell Gabo's talker credentials, and Dell Gabo will take over your credentials and former role at the Org. He will be your boss and he'll be give you further instructions when you meet with him for your weekly updates. Do you understand, Ms. Smith?"

'Gaby' nodded. What else could she do at that moment? She had to play along, but she planned to keep looking for a way to get her identity back.

"This is a real change for you, we know," Audrey said, "but try to look at it as a new opportunity, or even as therapy. It's an opportunity to work on your 'power control challenge disorder'. You are no longer obligated to play the 'mean bitch of a boss' role, and you will get to spend more time with your daughter—not to mention me and Gomez." At this Audrey smiled. Then she added, "I hope you enjoy spending real time with us losers and misfits instead of just spying from a distance. Now, how about another drink, Gaby? Elroy and I will join you to drink to our new friendship."

CHAPTER 20

Dell entered the Org offices, dressed in suit and tie for his first day in his new job.

"Good morning, Mr. Gabo," said the security officer at the front.

"Good Morning, Jeb. How are you today?"

"Just fine. Your people are waiting for you in the conference room."

At the Org, credentials were everything. No one questioned Gabriela Smith's departure; if the computer had deleted her and added Dell, they felt assured there was a good reason.

Dell headed to the elevator. He assumed his meeting would be on the twelfth floor, next to his new office. *So far, so good*, he thought. It was going exactly as Audrey had said.

At his end, he had retained his own, personal identity and so was not disabled when it came to routine transactions to do with finances or living arrangements, but he had also assumed part of Gabriela Smith's identity—all her professional stats and connections, including her accounts. In this regard, he was the new boss, the top dog, the one who would decide who would be sanctioned, who would be tracked, and what changes would be made in Afterlife or Otherlife, though of course Audrey would have a say.

Mr. Fortin and Mr. Wang greeted Dell as he entered the office. If they were surprised at the change in management, they didn't show it.

"Good morning, gentlemen," said Dell. "Could you get me the updated Afterlife and Otherlife files? I need to look at some of changes in the last 24 hours."

"We'll get them to you right away, Mr. Gabo."

"Are Mr. Sanchez and Ms. Singh in the conference room?"

"Yes, they're there waiting for you with the information you requested."

Dell went into his office, looked out the window and checked and messages on his mobile. He then picked up a coffee at the newly installed espresso machine just outside his office door and made his way to the conference room.

"Good morning Mr. Sanchez, good morning Ms. Singh," he said.

"Good morning Mr. Gabo," they said in unison. "We're ready to report."

PART 2

THE NEW REGIME

CHAPTER 21

"Have you had any experience parking cars?" asked the interviewer.

"No, I was a painter by trade, but I had to give it up due to allergies," said Gomez.

Gomez had applied for an offline job as a parking attendant, at Audrey's request. Since Dell had modified his age in the mainframe to 63 instead of 68, he no longer had to use a walker and helmet when he left his house. Gomez wanted 59, but Audrey explained that, unfortunately, he would never pass for 59.

He was wearing a clean white shirt buttoned to the top, dark, dressy jeans, and walking shoes. Audrey had told him to make sure he looked clean, dependable and like someone who could stand being out in all kinds of weather, rather than a construction worker or a clerk.

"I think I'm ready for a job where I can get some fresh air, interact with people, and keep things running smoothly," he said. "It's exactly the kind of job I'm looking for."

"What would you do, Mr. Gomez, if there were more cars than parking spaces available?" asked the tall, weight enhanced man in his forties who had introduced himself as Bill Sittler, head of Human Resources. He was wearing a bright red tie and his black hair was obviously dyed.

"I would simply and politely give them my regrets and explain that, unfortunately, they either need to find alternative parking or come back in 15 minutes when there might be space."

Gomez had actually looked forward to this interview. He'd run through the probable questions with Audrey and they had brainstormed the best answers. He felt confident, and he was happy to be participating in his offline life in a familiar way. He had liked working once.

And while he'd wanted a younger age, age 63 was okay with him—who wouldn't want to knock five years off their age? Audrey had assured him that if he took better care of himself, and worked out a little, he might be able to further lower his 'official' age, or only 'age' once every two years. He liked the idea of being in a position to enjoy the best of both worlds—mature and distinguished offline (if he worked at it), and as young and vigorous as he'd been 40 years ago online.

"How do you see your responsibilities?" asked Bill. "What is the extent of your job? Do you only point out parking spaces?"

"Oh, no," said Gomez, putting on the serious but confident face he had practiced with Audrey. "My job is not to simply park cars; my job is to enhance the shopping experience of each customer," he said.

As he answered, he sussed Bill out because Audrey had explained it was important to get a good idea of the interviewer as quickly as possible. "Is he or she a stickler for rules? A little laissez-faire, or what?" she'd said. "Check the dress, neatness, whether their finger nails are clipped and clean. Do they sit up straight, lean back? Create a profile in your mind and then answer according to what you think that person wants to hear."

Bill's red tie and dyed hair indicated a strong concern for other people's opinions. Audrey would say he was more interested in *appearing* to make the right decisions than actually making them and that he could be easily influenced. This, Audrey would like.

Gomez smoothly continued, "I know I only have a minor role in their shopping experience, but I am often the first and last contact a customer has at Shop Op. I can maximize their experience by helping them find the nearest parking spot, answering their questions and making appropriate suggestions, as necessary. I can even help them carry and load groceries. Basically, as a parking attendant my role is to be helpful and friendly and to make them feel like the team at Shop Op is doing the very best we possibly can."

Bill tightened his tie and gave Gomez a wide smile, "Mr. Gomez, I think you are exactly the person we're looking for," he said. "Congratulations. When do you think you can start? We need someone immediately."

"I can start tomorrow, if you want," Gomez said. "I can be here at eight-thirty, just before you open."

"Great! I really like your attitude, Mr. Gomez. Do you have any questions concerning compensation, hours, schedule or time for online activities?"

"I guess I would like a copy of my schedule and the hours you need me to work," said Gomez. "I'm aware of the hourly rate and benefits, as I read it in the job descriptions."

"Excellent," said Bill. "Your hours will be 9:00 a.m. to 1:00 p.m. It's five hours per day, five days per week. Sunday and Monday, you're off. Oh, and when you arrive, enter through the side door—here's the code to enter," he said, handing him a Shop Op employee card with a code on it.

"If you have any questions, you'll either find me in my office doing working employee records or payroll, or at the back of the store putting produce on the selves. We all do our bit here at Shop Op. Can I call you by your first name, Albert, or do you prefer Al?"

"Most people just call me Gomez, but Al is good."

"Okay then, Al. I'll see you tomorrow morning, bright and early. And remember, this is an offline job so we'd appreciate you *staying* offline as much as possible during work hours. You can check your online persona or messages during your breaks, if you like, but please use discretion. Take your breaks when it's not busy. We've had many problems with employees going online and neglecting their duties.

CHAPTER 22

Gomez entered the bistro from the back through the outdoor patio, and joined Audrey and Elroy at one of the tables in the far corner.

"So, how did it go?" asked Audrey, taking a sip of beer.

"I got the job and I start tomorrow," Gomez said, pleased with himself.

"Fantastic—let's drink to that. It's on Audrey," said Elroy raising his glass of beer to Gomez. "That means it's a go-to move on illegals. Are we still keeping it to the beef wieners, gluten buns and processed cheese? How about peanuts, I got a whole bin of them to get rid of!"

"Peanuts go well with hotdogs and they are only restricted, not illegal like meat products. We can move them easily. That and the hot dogs. It's hard for the vegan and allergy patrols to spot hot dogs, because we can disguise them to look like veggie products."

She looked at Gomez. "Did I mention we've laid our hands on a container full of 100 percent pure beef wieners—not just *any* wieners, but 100 percent pure beef? We've got them in cold storage, labeled 'vegan'," said Audrey. Then she looked at Elroy and asked, "Elroy, are those secret hot dog parties we discussed coming together? Those parties and the bistros—that's where the demand is."

"I'm in contact with the guy who organizes the parties, and we'll be meeting later right here in this bistro. The cameras will play the recording you made last week, so we should be in the clear. We just have to make sure everyone is aware of the danger. Also, we'll have a real problem if anyone is celiac—the buns are full of gluten, the real stuff—100 percent processed. Nothing is natural, except for the beef."

"And that's what our customers want," said Audrey.

"We just have to work out the means of payment and profit percentages," said Elroy.

"If they have paper dollars, they can pay with that," Audrey said. "Otherwise, I'll run the payment through a few bistros we've got on board. We're paying them off in hot dogs, peanuts, and processed toppings. This is how the money breaks down: 60 percent for expenses, such as purchase price and transport; 40 percent for us. The bistros mark up the sales price by 50 percent, so that's how they make their money, plus they take 5 percent on electronic transfers. It should be good for everyone."

"That sounds fair," Elroy said. "Like you say, everyone wins. Besides, it's mostly a question of principal—let's keep up the disturbing, and fuck up the do-gooders. To the disturbers!" he said, and lifted his beer for a toast.

"To the disturbers," joined in Audrey and Gomez.

Audrey turned and smiled at Gomez, "Okay, Gomez, so the plan is for you to set aside two parking spaces, one for Elroy and one for our clients. The clients will show up at the Shop Op and park beside Elroy. Then they will pick up a cart and go in buy some groceries. When they come out with the bags, you will exchange the bags for the ones in Elroy's trunk. The cameras can't pick up anything if you are blocked from the southeast corner. You work from 9:00 a.m. to 1:00 p.m., right?"

"Yeah, I plan to arrive around 8:30 a.m. to be ready, and I'll be in the parking lot until 1:00 p.m.," said Gomez. "I'm pretty flexible with my break times. He told me I can take them when I want as long as I'm not neglecting customers. My schedule seems pretty flexible, but I'll know more once I start working."

"Okay, around 11:00 a.m. is the best time for us to make our move," Audrey said. "There will be lots of customers in the store, but the parking lot won't be full. Remember, Elroy can't stay parked for too long in that lot or it will look suspicious." Then Audrey smiled at Gomez and said, "Oh yeah, and congrats for acing the interview. You are the key to this operation."

Gomez smiled. "Thanks," he said. Then he asked, "Do we have just one container?"

"For the moment, yes, but Estaban has a line on another, plus another load of peanuts. Maybe we can distribute them at the same time. Hotdogs, with peanuts and beer as an appetizer ... sounds pretty good, doesn't it? Through his new job with the Org, Dell can get us a line on more products as soon as Org agents confiscate more contraband."

"Great," said Gomez. "We're in business."

Audrey continued, "Remember, meat isn't totally illegal in some places. There's still some resistance to Org jurisdiction in the rural areas, so that is an avenue of supply we can consider if our sources dry up. Any questions or concerns?" she asked.

There wasn't.

"Okay," said Audrey. "Next time, the whole gang meets in Heaven Number 6. When we need to meet as a whole group, it's best that we meet online—except for you, Elroy since you don't have a fixed avatar. I'll brief you, though. And remember, no direct reference to wieners, peanuts, Shop Op, or any offline terms. Keep it Heaven-like. We'll work out the code words as we go along."

"What about Jan?"

"Gomez, you know that Jan is just a database—a good one, a compliant one, but just a database. She will be there, she will support you in your position and ideas and she will be a really good check for all of us, because if we get off script she'll let us know—it won't jive with her database. I'm more and more thankful for Jan and how we set that up."

Max said, "Me too."

Audrey added, "By the way, the three of us can continue to meet here for offline chit chats—we're good bistro people. Elroy, you can still meet with Estaban and Liliane in the park as well. Basically, with Dell in Gabriela Smith's job, we can meet much more easily, but we still have to be careful. By the way, do Estaban and Liliane still have their dog walking gig?"

"Yeah," Elroy said, "but Liliane had to find a new client. That cute little dog named Slug died. Apparently their kid fed him something and he choked. It's very sad. Liliane really liked that dog."

"Too bad," said Gomez, "but dogs don't really live that long anyway. It's better to have a cat or a bird. Parrots can outlast humans sometimes. I knew someone who *inherited* a parrot and it lived for another 20 years. Nobody knew how old it was, but some said it was almost a hundred."

Audrey interrupted. "Okay, so we're set for tomorrow. Elroy, you have the vehicle?"

Elroy nodded, and Audrey said, "The clients are set up to arrive at 15-minute intervals. They will park right next to you, facing the same direction. No backing into the parking space."

"Sounds good," said Gomez. "Do we have time for another beer?"

"Why not—this is worth celebrating."

CHAPTER 23

Dell sat in the conference room. He was leaning back in his chair, looking out the windows, waiting for Mr. Sanchez and Ms. Singh to arrive for their daily meeting.

Dell always arrived first so he could get the chair that adjusted, swung easily in both directions, and that he could lean back in. He had it set for just the right height. He could set his coffee cup off to the right of his laptop, and easily pick it up and take a sip with little effort. As far as he could tell Mr. Sanchez and Ms. Singh were not even aware of the chair's advantages.

In a few moments, Mr. Sanchez arrived, with Ms. Singh behind him. "Mr. Gabo," said Mr. Sanchez, "are we planning to complete the interdiction of peanuts completely? I think we should. There are rumours about an increase in clandestine peanut parties. They are calling them 'peanut dare parties'."

"I've heard the same," added Ms. Singh. "I've heard that it is very dangerous. Nobody has died yet, but it's just a question of time. We've had dare parties in the past, such as swim parties without lifejackets, or bike rides without helmets; but those were mostly adolescent affairs. Children we didn't immediately censure stopped such behaviour when they became adults. But this is totally different. First of all, the participants are often adults, and some are even seniors! Second, they appear to have an attraction to the danger itself. This could create serious social problems, sir!"

Mr. Sanchez jumped in, "Yes, in the past people did crazy activities because they didn't understand the danger and the *thrill/risk ratio* was not widely known. Now, it's totally irresponsible. Peanut allergies can be fatal. It has to stop."

At Dell's lack of reaction, Mr. Sanchez went on tried again.

"Apparently, they sit around a table with a bowl of peanuts and an epi-pen auto injector, and wait to see if anyone is allergic. Can you imagine? I think this is just a way to show disrespect to the safety measures the Org has put in place to protect people. It must be one of those 'disturber' things. Disturbers love carrying out antisocial acts."

Dell nodded, as if considering their words. Ms. Singh said, "Mr. Gabo, we need to act. Peanuts can no longer be considered simply 'restricted' or 'forbidden without prescription'. Peanut possession should be both illegal and punishable."

Dell sighed. "I understand your concern and I agree with your opinions, both about the danger and the motives for holding peanut parties," he said. "However, I have to point out that peanuts are presently tolerated in bistros that serve alcoholic drinks. It seems like it would be a major operation to inspect all the bistros while trying to enforce such a law."

"But I think it's *necessary*," said Ms. Singh.

"We'd only create a lot of frustration for the challenged and non techs, who are the ones who frequent the bistros. We can't afford to stir them up. We have nothing to pacify them with—offline religion bores them and they're not interested in being online. Besides, it seems their lifestyles lead to strong immunities; studies show that most non techs are not allergic to peanuts."

Mr. Sanchez saw most things as either black or white and he did not like this grey area Dell was describing, though Ms. Singh was leaning toward what Dell was saying.

Not about to give up easily, Mr. Sanchez said, "If we don't clamp down on peanuts, there is a high possibility that someone with a peanut allergy may accidentally consume one, with dire consequences. I am receiving a lot a pressure from the Association of Right to Life Allergy Free. They are powerful, and they are increasingly allied with the vegan associations. The two of them combined forces to prohibit dairy, and when the vegans conceded on the gluten free bread issue, their alliance got even stronger."

"I understand," said Dell, "Their argument is that people can live as they wish to online, but that offline dangers should be strictly managed. They are quite right when they say that saving the life of one cow, or the health of a human with an allergy, is worth a little frustration and discomfort."

Ms. Singh interjected, "Do you think, Mr. Gabo, that part of the peanut problem has to do with some of these disturber groups? Perhaps that's where we need to focus."

"That's a possibility, Ms. Singh. That is why I would like you and Mr. Sanchez to look into it and keep me updated."

"Should we create a task force on it?" asked Mr. Sanchez, obviously delighted with the added responsibility and the chance to go after something so dear to his philosophical outlook.

"Yes, Mr. Sanchez, a task force should be formally designated."

"Who would lead the task force?"

"Why not you, Mr. Sanchez?" suggested Dell. Then, to pacify Ms. Singh, he said, "You will be a member. Ms. Singh, and I will keep you in mind to lead another task force in the future."

Dell rested his elbows on the table and looked back and forth from Sanchez to Singh as sternly as possible. He said, "About the peanuts, I understand your concerns, but as I pointed out, bistros are frequented by those who have no online life, and if beer and peanuts keep them from becoming agitated, I think that's a positive. Let's not make the same mistake we made with vaping and cigarettes. We ended up creating a black market, and the disturbers gained more influence."

"But what happens if someone who has been brought up properly, in a sanitized, clean, proper environment comes into the bistro and is exposed to peanut dander? There is a real danger someone could get sick or die, and then the Org will be accused of not foreseeing the problem and anticipating the danger."

"Bistros are required to ensure their patrons know that they are not peanut free," said Dell. "They post signs and put warnings on their menus."

"Do you really think that is strong enough?" asked Mr. Sanchez. "I would prefer they hang signs on their doors that say something like, 'danger, beware of peanuts'."

Dell sat back in his chair. There was probably a reasonable compromise. As Audrey had pointed out, if they were to make good money trafficking peanuts and hot dogs, then they would have to create a market for contraband by clamping down. Dell would have to look like he saw peanut parties as a problem and be willing to come down hard on certain aspects of the illegal peanut trade … as long as it didn't interrupt the flow of the group's side business, of course. Besides, the upside of making the bistros put signs on their doors was customers would know they could get peanuts inside the establishment. It was actually an effective marketing strategy.

"Okay, team—let's go with that," he said. "And keep me up to date on whatever you learn about the disturbers."

Recently, Dell had seen a tightening of regulations on meat and allergenic substances. Among allergenics, peanuts had long been a point of contention between the vegans and the Right to Life Allergy Free group. For the vegans, they were a source of protein, but for the Right to Life Allergy Free group, they were lethal. The compromise was that peanuts became a controlled substance that required a special license in order to purchase them.

Bistros—which mostly served non tech and challenged groups—were not exempt, but they were largely ignored when it came to enforcing this regulation. This pretty much solidified the allergy and vegan groups into an alliance that fought against contraband peanuts, among other things. They had long ago browbeat run-of-the-mill vegetarians into giving up milk, eggs and other dairy products, as both vegan and allergy activists saw thought of these foods as triggers.

Then meat wound up on the chopping block, lead by the vegan group, but supported by the Right to Life Allergy Free group. It was probably some sort of political deal; the vegans had supported the Right to Life Allergy Free group in their stand against gluten.

All this food regulation had become somewhat problematic for the Org. A lot of resources were now allocated to controlling the illegal trade of meat, dairy and eggs offline, while at the same time further resources were used to provide sanctuaries online for those who enjoyed these things. It was hard to reconcile prohibiting something offline and allowing it or, as some said, promoting it, online. It was considered immoral by the vegans, and their pressure tactics to ban virtual animal products online as well as offline were becoming increasingly persuasive.

Most Otherlife programs already prohibited meat consumption and, some treated all living eukaryotes as equal. More stringent programs even considered all prokaryotes to have equal rights.

Offline, it was impossible to live this way—everyone has to eat, no matter how fanatical they are about *what* they eat. Online, as all avatars were databases, it was easier to argue for banning eating. Databases do not require the intake of living organisms to remain viable; eating was more of a social concession than anything else.

Heaven Number 6 allowed for the consumption of just about anything, and since the introduction of alcohol and comfort food, the sky was the limit. The only restriction left was that Fridays had to be fish days. This was not a problem. It meant that white wine was served in the espresso bars on Fridays.

Dell wanted to make sure Audrey knew that Mr. Sanchez and Ms. Singh were investigating disturbers. Luckily, he had Kata back and, as part of the espresso gang, he had constant online communication with Audrey.

Dell was excited to talk to her because he was convinced the task force would be an asset. It would provide a wealth of information relating to prohibited substances, such as sources, connections, suppliers, and clients. Also, Audrey would be able to trace the task force's actions and if they got too close to finding out about the espresso gang, she could send them false leads.

CHAPTER 24

Gomez prepared breakfast, something he wasn't used to doing, as he usually started the day with two or three cups of coffee and ate later. However, it was his first day at the parking lot and he didn't know if he would have to eat later.

Should I pack sandwiches? Can I go into the Shop Op and get a prepackaged meal? He didn't know. He figured he needed to be prepared for whatever. The best thing to do was to fill up with breakfast and, if necessary, he would be able to tough it out until 1:00 p.m. when he finished work.

Gomez poured some syrup over the oatmeal he had prepared and sat down at his table. The weather was clear outside—it looked like it would be a nice day.

He went online to say 'hi' to Jan, but his concentration wasn't there. It was the first day on the job—both as a parking attendant and part of a ring of contraband food distributors.

When should I leave, he wondered? His transportation app indicated that he could take the 8:05 a.m. metro to get to work by 8:30 a.m., but he didn't want to take a chance of being late, not on his first day, so he decided to take an earlier one.

The metro was crowded. He got a seat next to a young female-identified. He sat down, looked at her and smiled. She didn't take her eyes off her mobile, though she shifted over to give him more space.

As his stop approached, he stood up and as close to the doors as possible. When they opened, he got off, went up the escalator and exited just as the sun was appearing above the building in front of the Shop Op. It was a short, easy walk, except for dodging pedestrians who were head down in their mobiles.

The parking lot was huge and there were almost no cars in it, except at the very back. He assumed they were employee cars.

Gomez made his way to the employees' entrance, entered his code, went inside, and picked up the yellow florescent vest he had to wear to identify him as a parking lot attendant. This was the closest he'd ever come to a uniform. It was a little big for him, but he could deal with it. Strangely, it made him feel important—powerful wouldn't be the right word, but there was a certain authority attached to the vest that he had never had before.

The morning went well and as planned, Elroy showed up at 11:00 a.m. and parked in the area they had agreed upon, neither too far away to be conspicuous, nor too near to make it impossible for their clients to make the transfer.

Elroy acknowledged Gomez as discreetly as possible and then went into the building with his shopping cart. No more than five minutes later, a woman driving a hybrid SUV drove up, gave the 'little finger on the steering wheel wave' signal, and Gomez had her park next to Elroy's car.

"Can I help you with those bags, ma'am? They look heavy," he said politely.

"Why certainly, sir—that would be very kind," the lady replied with a twinkle in her eye.

Gomez opened Elroy's trunk as he placed the bags on the ground behind the woman's trunk. The two trunks were less than a metre apart. He opened the igloo in Elroy's trunk, while the woman opened her igloo. The wieners were transferred, and one of the lady's bags was placed in Elroy's trunk. A bag of non-gluten free buns was then transferred to the lady's trunk, along with the remaining bags on the ground … and the deed was done.

As the woman drove out, another car followed Gomez's directions and parked in the same spot, the same way. Gomez recognized the driver as the bartender at the bistro he, Elroy and Audrey most often met at. Neither acknowledged each other, as instructed; only a friendly smile among strangers and the little finger signal. Audrey and Dell were strict on this. Acquaintance recognition should only happen one in ten times at the most. Statistically, nobody has that many offline acquaintances. Cameras that caught more frequent recognition patterns would trigger an algorithm to send an alert.

Things carried on in much the same way until the last client had received his 100 percent beef wieners. Elroy came back for his car around 25 minutes after leaving it.

The next day's plan involved Estaban or Liliane making the drop, as Elroy's car would be picked up by an algorithm if he showed up too often. Luckily, they'd all frequented the Shop Op on a regular basis in the past, and statistically it was normal for people to shop in the same store up to three times a week; however, it was statistically very rare for someone to show up at Shop Op two days in a row.

When the hot dog transfers were over, Gomez did his regular job until 1:00 p.m. Later, he planned to meet with Max, Lyle, Hector, Kata and Walrus online, so everyone could analyze how their first day went, and where they could improve. Audrey would brief Elroy later at the bistro.

CHAPTER 25

Heaven Number 6 started to change considerably. Kata was slowly modifying the ambience of the place to the espresso gang's tastes. Besides the introduction of alcoholic drinks and comfort food snacks in the espresso bars, music was no longer exclusively religious. Soft pop was now intermingled with Christian rock. As of yet there was no hard-rock allowed, but there were demands for it as well as for rap and slam.

The colour red, once prohibited, was beginning to appear here and there, and gospel choirs were punctuating the Archangel Gabriel's sermons, which made church far more uplifting. Lyle insisted they take it slow so that the changes weren't too jarring. They didn't want too many people asking questions; above all, they needed to protect their offline business.

All and all, it was a livelier place and was gaining popularity as an Afterlife program under Kata's careful management. When Audrey had reinstated Kata for Dell, she designed her to have many of the social skills Dell felt he lacked. He'd asked Audrey for someone with charm and the ability to win others over, and he was very satisfied with Kata, Version II.

That night, it was an excited group who met in their favourite online espresso bar for a status update. "Well, Max," said Lyle "Everything seems under control—completely organized and running well."

"It's running like a charm, Lyle," Max said. "And how are things from your perspective?"

"Heaven Number 6 is really evolving," Lyle said. "Kata is making some really exceptional changes that are making the place so much better."

"I'm doing my best," piped in Kata. "It's going to be interesting here, the best of all the afterlives!"

Lyle smiled. "I'm glad to hear that." he said. "Hector and Walrus, how's procurement going?"

"We've got a line on some double-roasted peanuts," said Walrus excitedly. "People are going to love them. Elroy will pick them up tomorrow."

"Oh, those things are delicious, sweet *and* savoury" said Lyle.

Hector looked at Walrus with a worried frown and Walrus nodded.

"What is it?" asked Lyle.

"We've got some competition. Someone is undercutting our prices by mixing tofu with meat and selling for less. The problem is that it's creating doubt as to the purity of meat in general. Walrus thought we could get the Org to check it out."

"What do you think, Kata? Is there anything to be done? Could the task force on peanuts be expanded?

"I'll check it out," said Kata.

"Kata, anything else new coming up we should know about?"

"An Org program, led by me, of course, has proposed some promising lifestyle developments" said Kata. "They're going to allow pets in Heaven Number 6. Gabriel will be declaring that all vertebrates have a soul and will be admitted if accompanied by a human avatar."

"Just think—no dog poop to pick up" said Max, excitedly, thinking of his old black lab dog. He'd loved that dog.

"Well that gets me thinking about the market for contraband cat food," said Lyle. The others smiled.

The meeting wrapped up with a sense of satisfaction. Business was booming.

CHAPTER 26

"Al, could you come in here for a moment?"

"No problem, Mr. Sittler, how can I help you?"

"Call me Bill, Al—no need for formalities here."

"Okay, Bill."

"Al, we're going to need you to stock shelves today. We're behind. You can leave your vest here and give us a hand. Maria will show you what you need to do."

"What about the parking ... won't we have a problem?" asked Gomez, a little concerned.

"No, this is more important for the moment," said Bill.

Gomez felt slightly panicked. Estaban would be driving up soon. It was his first time as a courier, and Gomez didn't know if Estaban knew where to park. He had to get a message to Audrey. If he emailed or texted her, he would create an electronic trail that could be traced and used against them if they were ever investigated, but if he could get online, he could get to Lyle or Kata through Max. Hopefully Kata was in Number 6, and Dell could get through to Audrey, and maybe fix things.

He excused himself for a bathroom break and as soon as he was alone in a cubical he frantically searched for Kata online. Meanwhile, Estaban and Liliane drove in and saw there was no Gomez. *What happened,* they wondered? Estaban's first instinct was to contact Audrey, but Liliane reminded him that was a no-no.

They parked in the middle of the lot, where there was a space on each side. Their problem was that they didn't have a description of the customer's car model— Gomez had that.

"Well," said Liliane, "There's nothing we can do but the shopping. We have to just hope the customer knows more than we do."

"I doubt that. You know Audrey. She's a stickler for discretion, and only knowing what you need to know."

Estaban opened the latch on the trunk and they started walking toward the store.

Liliane whispered, "Estaban, what do you think happened to Gomez?"

"No bloody idea—let's just hope the gig isn't up."

When they got inside, Estaban and Liliane grabbed a cart and started going up and down the aisles, picking up some essentials, like toilet paper and soap. In aisle number five they found Gomez stocking various sauces and spices. He looked at them and then hunched his shoulders, trying to look like he hadn't noticed them. It wasn't easy; none of them had expected this, and they had no contingency plan.

Thinking fast, Gomez took a couple of steps closer to them. "Can I help you? Are you looking for something?"

"No," said Liliane. "We're just filling our list."

"That's good, because I'm not sure I can help you—my job is actually to be the parking lot attendant," Gomez said with an apologetic smile. "I'm not sure where everything is." Then he added, "By the way, I hope you didn't have any trouble finding a parking spot."

"No we're parked near the center—we could have parked closer, but we needed the exercise."

Gomez laughed. "You seem to be in great shape, ma'am," he said. "Not like a woman I saw recently in a green, hybrid sedan. She drove all over looking for a place to park. I thought she was trying to get close to the door, but maybe she was actually trying to get exercise too. She parked in in a far corner."

"Well, it's good to walk," Liliane smiled. Then she turned to Estaban and said. "Estaban could you get my wallet? I think I left it in the glove compartment. I'll continue getting the stuff on our list and meet you at the payout."

Estaban and Gomez knew exactly what Liliane meant, and Estaban went to look for the green sedan. He exited the Shop Op and checked the parking lot.

There were at least five green cars out there—was it forest green, florescent green, light green? *Shit, I need a better description than 'hybrid green sedan'*, he thought.

He looked around for someone who looked a little lost as he walked back to his and Liliane's car. Nobody looked more out of place than anyone else. He frowned. He didn't even know if their customer would be male- or female-identified, weight enhanced or what. There was not much he could do but go back, pay, and leave. *This might be a write-off,* he thought.

CHAPTER 27

Audrey and Elroy sat at their usual table drinking a beer and enjoying a small bowl of tamari peanuts. "It feels good to know that these are *our* peanuts, don't you think Audrey?"

"Yeah, it's nice … but we have a major problem," she replied. "Who would think they'd take a parking lot attendant and put him to work stacking shelves? What if it happens again?"

"You're right," said Elroy, leaning back and taking a gulp of beer, then downing a fist full of peanuts. "It's something we didn't plan for."

"Gomez said he had no choice—it was either move with it or risk losing his job. If he lost his job, we'd be out of a parking lot attendant and our whole scheme would be up shit creek."

"Here comes Gomez now," noted Elroy.

"Hi," said Gomez. "So it looks like I fucked up, heh?" he asked, smiling, as he set his beer on the table.

Audrey laughed. "Let's just say we're weren't as smart as we thought we were. But all's well that end's well. I'm sure it won't be our last stumble."

"So, what's the plan?" asked Gomez. "Are these peanuts for everyone?" he further asked, looking at the snacks.

"Help yourself," said Elroy, handing Gomez the bowl.

Audrey leaned back and frowned, clearly concentrating. Then she said, "Okay. First, is there a way this can work for us? Maybe having Gomez inside Shop Op from time to time can be useful. This is way out there … but maybe there's a way we could use Shop Op to distribute—they've got cold storage, shelving, docking, the whole bloody works. Can you imagine if our customers could simply walk in and buy not only beef wieners and peanuts, but dairy products, processed goods, the whole works?"

Gomez stopped with a fistful of peanuts to his mouth. "Come again?" he asked.

"When was the last time most people had a processed cheese slice?" she asked wistfully. "Gomez is the only one at this table who can remember when that was considered food. I have a vague recollection of trying one when I was a child. I loved it. I bet this bistro is full of people who would die for an old-style grilled cheese sandwich—processed cheese melted between fried, white bread."

Elroy laughed. "Sounds amazing," he said.

A light came into Audrey's eyes. "Listen guys," she said. "I have a plan and I think I know who can help us execute it. We need to run that Shop Op—manage it completely."

CHAPTER 28

"Come in, Gaby," Audrey said as her talker knocked on the door.

"Good afternoon, Audrey. How are we this afternoon?" asked Gabriela Smith, former bigshot at the Org ... and now Audrey's talker.

"Excellent," Audrey said. "I was wondering why I didn't see you last week. Was there a problem?"

"I'm sorry, but when it's my week for my daughter, sometimes I get tied up. I contacted the Org to say I couldn't make it. Didn't they inform you?"

"Yeah, Mr. Gabo contacted me personally. It's good to have contacts in the right places," Audrey replied, adding coyly, "but you remember those days, don't you?"

"I certainly do—and I'm not sure I miss them, Audrey," replied Gaby with a tight smile. "You were right about that. My offline life is much nicer than I ever thought it could be. I appreciate that you and Dell kept my salary at the same level. How can I complain? I don't have to work so hard, and I have lots of money and a beautiful apartment, plus I get to spend more time with my daughter. I miss my online life a little though, and was hoping you could get me an avatar, Audrey."

"I'll have Mr. Gabo check into it," Audrey said. "I'd like to propose that we continue our session at the local bistro—the one Elroy and I met you at … you know, where we explained your new role and identity. What do you think—are you up for it?"

"Why not, I'm a talker and I can talk anywhere," Gaby said.

Audrey went to closet and got her walker. Despite the success she and her group were having, she felt it would be prudent to continue to be 'challenged' when seen with Gaby. She admired and respected her intelligence but she didn't trust her.

"Shall we be off, Gaby?" she asked.

Gaby nodded. They took the elevator to the lobby and then went down the street to the corner, where the local bistro was located. It was still early when they got there, and there were not many people in the bistro.

A table by the window, with the patio view, was open. They sat down and Audrey ordered a beer. "What would you like, Gaby?"

"A beer is fine. I prefer a lager."

"Great," Audrey said, and ordered her one. Then she asked, "Listen, Gaby. Would you like some peanuts?"

"Is that prudent?"

"What is prudent and what isn't?" Audrey asked enigmatically, "Anyway, peanuts are restricted—but not illegal."

"Then why not, Audrey? I don't have an allergy, so why not?"

"Have you had anything illegal?" Audrey asked. If Gaby was surprised by the question, she didn't show it.

"Not to my knowledge. As you remember, until you and your friends displaced me, I made a career out of being pretty straight. I obeyed the rules, and, as you know, I enforced them."

"What would you say if I ordered two hotdogs?"

"Why not? I'm a little hungry."

"No, I mean *real* hotdogs—100 percent pure beef, on gluten-laced buns, with processed cheese, mustard and real ketchup. In other words, the real thing, and 100 percent illegal, with no natural ingredients, except maybe the beef."

"Are you trying to get me into trouble, Audrey? Why would you do that? I've been good about the changes. I'm no longer Ms. Smith. I'm Gaby the talker, single mother and regular gal, and nothing more."

"Ms. Smith, Gabriela, Gaby—you can be all of them," said Audrey, adding "I'm going to have a real, 100 percent beef hotdog—totally illegal—right here … and I'm asking you if you want one."

"Audrey, I haven't had one since I was an adolescent," said Gaby. "My parents used to barbeque. I hardly remember what they taste like. They called it junk food back then, but I remember us kids loved them. We probably didn't feel so well if we ate too much, though," she laughed, "but I have fond memories of hotdogs."

"Well, then, let's go for it! What do we have to lose? The cameras are off voice and are only on facial, and 100 percent beef looks pretty much the same as a vegan dog to the cameras."

Tempted, Gaby said, "Okay, I guess it couldn't hurt."

Audrey got up and, with her walker, went to the bar to order. She stopped in the washroom to text Dell and Elroy, and then went back to the table.

"They're on their way," she told Gaby as she sat down. I ordered mustard, cheese, and relish for both."

"You're in charge," said Gaby.

Gabriela wasn't sure how she felt about a 100 percent, pure beef hotdog. She, like many, was vegan without the philosophy or the conviction. She understood that keeping animals in close quarters for slaughter was not an ethical thing to do, so it was easy to go along with the belief system about the immorality of such cruelty, which in turn made it easy to enforce the laws that had been put into place to appease vegan pressure groups. Rules were rules, and she both obeyed and enforced them—or at least organized the means for the culprits to be caught. Now here she was with Audrey, ready to break those very rules.

Audrey looked across at Gaby. *How will she react to the hotdogs,* she wondered? *Will she show her true feelings?* Audrey knew she was dealing with Ms. Smith, Gabriela and Gaby—three distinct characters in one. She also knew that Gaby was not what she seemed. Her competence as the feared Ms. Smith had little to do with conviction, and more to do with simple efficiency and responsibility. She liked being good at her job. It made her feel powerful. Given this, Audrey was hoping, perhaps Gaby would come to see that she could be as good on one side of the moral coin as the other. If she could get her involved with the espresso gang's scheme, it would be perfect.

Gaby sensed what she was up to. "Okay, Audrey," she said. "I guess you've compromised me by having me eat meat. Now what is it you want from me?"

"How do you know I want something from you?"

"Audrey, you never do anything without an intention," she pointed out. "I've been your talker now for months. You didn't set it up for Dell and me to change places because you found me more appealing than Dell as a talker. So let's just be clear with each other. We are both intelligent people."

"You're right, Gabriela," said Audrey. "I have something to run by you, a kind of partnership or association proposal; something that will provide you with more income—*much* more income. Plus I can also get you an afterlife or otherlife of your choosing. Most of all, you'd be back to using your natural skills. I'm sure you miss using them, don't you, Gabriela?"

"I'm listening Audrey."

"Have you ever been to Shop Op?" asked Audrey.

"Of course—hasn't everyone?"

"Well, there's going to be an opening for a store manager at the one on Fifth Street. Gomez is working there as a parking attendant, as well as stocking shelves on occasion. Let's just say I have access to a supply of 100 percent beef wieners, and now I can also get beef hamburger patties. You tasted the product—it's damn good, isn't it?"

"Yes," Gabriela said cautiously. "As a matter of fact, I'd forgotten how much I missed that taste."

"Exactly," Audrey said. "Like most, you have gradually come to believe that the vegan stuff is as good as real meat, or even better. We've fallen for the Org propaganda. But it's not. Believe me … when people taste the real thing they want more. And when the carbs hit them, they have to *have* more. Right now we're only moving hotdogs, but as soon as we also start supplying hamburgers, demand will spike. This bistro has tripled its sales in the last month, just by providing hotdogs and peanuts."

Gabriela didn't overthink it. She wiped her mouth with a napkin and said, "You've convinced me Audrey.

But what does this have to do with the job at Shop Op?"

"Gabriela, I think you know. I have an ever-expanding clientele and we need a good, reliable distribution center. We need a place where our clients come for legal products so their facials don't attract suspicion. And we need someone with the skills to operate it, someone who knows how the Org. You're that someone."

"Ethically, I'm not sure I agree with what you're doing, Audrey," said Gabriela. "Animals have to be killed in order to supply meat products, and that's a violation of their rights as living beings."

"Isn't there an ethical question when destroying an eternal online persona?" countered Audrey. "Offline beings die anyway."

"You're referring to Dell losing his online persona, Kata, I presume?" asked Gabriela, arching one eyebrow.

Audrey didn't answer. She just said, "If I can assure you that the animals are well cared for, free range, would that influence you?"

"What about my responsibilities as a talker? Eventually someone will discover the double role."

"Here's the beauty of the situation," said Audrey. "Not only will you be the store manager, but you will retain your talker job part time, and your participants will be only members of our little team; Gomez, me, Elroy—who you've met—plus two other members who you might remember from when you were Jan in Heaven Number 6—Hector and Walrus."

"Not bad, Audrey, not bad at all," said Gabriela. "I was impressed at how you got me eliminated from my Org job, but this is even *more* impressive. I see why you need me. You need someone with an intimate knowledge of Org investigations and surveillance. So, with my managerial skills I'm pretty much made to measure, right?" she chuckled.

"You're right. With you on board, we would have the team we need for a venture that will be both economically and personally rewarding. We're disturbers, Gabriela—and it can be both highly entertaining and lucrative. I think you'll find that breaking the rules is more fun that enforcing them. It requires more imagination. Apparently, they used to call it 'living on the edge'."

"I suppose I'll need to apply at Shop Op if I'm to get the job you're referring to? It can't be automatic. They don't know me."

"Don't worry, we did a Dell on them. Their present manager will find that his offline persona has been modified, and he's now working the storeroom at another Shop Op. You are the new manager. Your facial, identity, position and office are all there waiting for you. A Mr. Bill Sittler, your H.R. person, will be there to meet you and show you around. He's not in the loop and not part of the team."

"Wow," said Gabriela.

Audrey added, "Keep an eye on him—he's in charge of Gomez's work load. Gomez thinks he won't be a problem, so for the moment we'll leave things as they are."

"Okay," said Gabriela.

"We'll want Gomez controlling the parking lot, the docking, and the shelving, as you'll see. You may want to change things to be more efficient, and Gomez is cool with that. He's not too interested in anything but upgrading his offline lifestyle. In other words, he's not interested in managing anything the way you, me, and Dell are. His ego isn't as dependant on control and superiority, as our egos are."

"I understand," said Gabriela. "I suppose I keep in touch through my talker meetings?"

"Yeah, but it would be good for you to have an online presence in Heaven Number 6 as well. I thought about giving you Jan again, but Gomez likes the Max-Jan relationship too much. Maybe you could come in as an assistant to the archangel? You could be the Angel Peter, and you can choose an online avatar separate from us as well. Dell will set it up for you, through me. It's not a good idea for you and Dell to have offline contact."

"On the Heaven Number 6 subject, what if I became one of the angels who runs your espresso bar? That would correspond well to my manager responsibilities at Shop Op. It would also make it easy to express concerns using code, which I'm sure you're using already."

"I like that idea—that's perfect, and you'll look good in wings," said Audrey, happy to see that Gabriela was already on track and ready to take on responsibilities. The only thing left to do was to talk about percentages and how they would be distributed.

"Okay," Gabriela said. "I'll be Annie, no wings, in my twenties and a little outspoken—a bit of a pain. That'll give me room to say just about anything. I'd like Annie to be my real avatar, not just for the team. If one day she decides to move to an Otherlife, I want that too. I've never had a personal avatar. Mine have always been for Org purposes."

"Annie it is," said Audrey. "And on another subject, you probably haven't seen any paper money for a while, but we compensate each other in paper, crypto-currency, and credit at certain merchants and suppliers. I decide who gets what, but I try to keep it as even as possible, depending on workload, responsibilities, and danger of the job."

Gabriela nodded.

"Yours will be a pivotal role—like mine and Dell's. As a Shop Op manager and part-time talker, your income status will increase in the Org database, so you'll be able to upgrade your standard of living without the Org noticing and questioning where the money's coming from—not that they're capable of that anyway. Sometimes they get lucky, though."

"I'm sure we can work it all out as we go, Audrey," said Gabriela."

"Right. So I take it we have a deal?"

"We have a deal. I'm in. I'm in 100 percent."

The two women smiled at each other and slowly finished their beer and peanuts. This was a better system than the parking lot scheme. The potential was so much greater now, and both of them could see that.

CHAPTER 29

Gabriela walked back to her apartment. It was a beautiful day and she decided to go via the park. It was amazing how nice it was, and how few people took advantage of it. Online life had become more important for most people, and little use was made of parks. Only non techs and the challenged used them much. Here and there, Gabriela could see people sitting on benches, talking as normal, well-adjusted members of society walked by with their heads in their mobiles, half offline, half online. She wondered who was having a nicer life, and suspected it was the ones on the benches.

Gabriela had largely had her head in her phone until she lost her online status. She was looking forward to having a new online persona; however, she promised herself she would continue to enjoy simple offline joys.

As she approached her home, she suddenly remembered that she had her daughter this week. Sarah would be at the apartment, probably online in her own afterlife or otherlife. As Ms. Smith, department head at the Org, she could easily have pried into her daughter's avatar activities and contacts, but she didn't. She remained in the dark about her daughter's choices, feeling firmly that it was none of her business, though it would be nice to know what Sarah was up to, if only to know her daughter better.

"Hi, Sarah," she said as she entered the apartment.

Sarah looked up and put an index finger in the air which meant, 'just a minute'—a minute that would be a good half hour or more.

"No problem, I'll start supper—fried eggplant with a tomato bean sauce tonight."

She thought her daughter would appreciate the meal and she knew it had the protein and vitamin content recommend by the Org, after all, it was out of the authorized recipe ebook.

"Why can't we have some meat once in a while?" moaned Sarah. "I've had it with my friends—it's not harmful and it's *so* good."

Gabriela thought about the hotdog she had eaten. When Sarah was born, she had promised herself that her daughter would never know the taste of meat or processed food, yet it appeared she'd tried it anyway.

"Where did you get meat, Sarah? You know it's illegal. You can get in big trouble with the Org if you're caught."

"Everybody eats it—lots of my friends do. We get it in the park, or behind the school."

"Don't you dare buy meat from the park! If you want meat, I'll get it for you. I don't approve, but at least I know where to get meat that is pure and not mixed with all kinds of crap."

"How can *you* get it? You wouldn't know where to buy it, mom."

"Don't worry Sarah, I can get it—that's all you have to know. From now on, I will have some here for you, but I don't want you getting it from outside."

Sarah looked satisfied and for once quite happy with her mother, a situation that had become quite rare lately.

Gabriela poured herself a glass of white wine and contemplated her new life. Gabriela Anne Smith was poised for a big change and she was looking forward to managing something besides her own life. Would she be able to work with Audrey? She thought so, at least for a while—then maybe other opportunities would open themselves up. *Who knows,* thought Gabriela?

The future looked a lot different than it had this morning. Audrey's comment about her ego being the type that needed to be in control and have a sense of superiority was true. She laughed to herself and thought, *why not?* If that's who she was, then that's who she was.

CHAPTER 30

"Hello, Ms. Smith, my name is Bill Sittler. I believe you are the new head manager. Your profile is highly impressive and it will be an honour working for you. I'm sure you know Shop Op better than me, but would you like me to give you the tour of this Shop Op, or would you prefer to do that later? I know you have a lot of things to do. I'm available for you when you need me," Bill said, deferring to his new boss.

"Thanks, Mr. Sittler. There is one thing you could do. Could you bring me a list of the employees and their responsibilities, please?"

"Call me Bill, Ms. Smith."

"Thanks but I'm going to stay with 'Mr. Sittler'. I prefer a certain formality in the workplace."

"Certainly, Ms. Smith. And if you wait just a minute, I will give you access to the list you asked for."

Bill fiddled for a moment with his mobile and Gabriela heard her computer screen ping. A link and password appeared, and she entered the program. She took a long look at the employee list on her screen while Mr. Sittler remained standing in front of her. Finally, she said, "We have an Albert Gomez here who seems to function as both as a parking attendant and stocker-stacker—is that the case, Mr. Sittler?"

"Yes, he was hired as a parking attendant but we're understaffed and so I thought it appropriate to pull him off the parking lot during slacker times. It seemed a better use of the resource."

"That was a good decision, Mr. Sittler. I like initiative. Could you send Mr. Gomez in to see me in five minutes, please?"

"Of course," said Bill, and then he retreated.

Gabriela texted Audrey to tell her she would be meeting with Gomez, and Audrey texted her back immediately. The plan was that, after the first few minutes of the meeting, Audrey would remotely manipulate the camera feed so it showed an empty office so that Gabriela and Gomez could talk more seriously and in private.

"So, Gaby—it's strange to see you outside your talker role," said Gomez when he walked into her office. "Now you're my boss. I guess I should call you 'Ms. Smith' from now on."

"I'll still see you from time to time as your talker," Gaby said. "There, I can continue to be Gaby. Here, obviously Ms. Smith would be best. Actually, as I just told Mr. Sittler, I prefer to be addressed formally and so everyone here needs to call me Ms. Smith."

"I heard from Dell that the old Ms. Smith was not to be tangled with," laughed Gomez.

"The new Ms. Smith is not to be tangled with either," smiled Gabriela.

"So, we need to set up the work, I guess. You're going to tell me what I am supposed to do, as well as where and when, right?"

"That's right. For the moment, your schedule will be the same, but you'll be spending less time in the parking lot. Elroy will direct trunk to trunk sales from the corner while selling his park boat tours, which I have given him permission to do, and Estaban and Liliane will take turns driving. I can control the cameras, with Audrey's help, from here. You will be working the dock, stacking the buns and dogs. You need to put the '100 percent natural ingredients' stickers on each package. The brand name will be 'Health Op'. Your part requires a lot of physical work—do you think you're up for it?"

"I can handle it. Besides, Audrey says that if I get into better shape, I can lose a few years."

"You don't look a day over 70," laughed Gabriela, "Just kidding, Gomez—you're looking better all the time."

"Thanks, Gaby."

"Anyway, as soon as the volume increases, we can bring in help. Apparently you guys have some certified mentally challenged friends that would be up for it."

"Most of our team and friends have some kind of challenged certificate. Elroy has one."

"I know that, but we need Elroy where he is. According to Audrey, nobody knows the offline underworld like Elroy, and we need someone who can identify who might be a spy or snitch."

"Apparently you know who the snitches are too," remarked Gomez.

"I used to recruit and organize them," admitted Gabriela, "but now I'm a little rusty. Too much time working as a talker brought out too much of the nice in me."

"We'll try to keep your nice out of sight of the wrong people," said Gomez. "We'll keep it for ourselves."

"Sounds good. Let's get busy. We've got a business to run. And Gomez? It would be a good strategy if you appeared not to like me too much in front of the other employees. Have a bit of an attitude around me—competent but not compliant. It'll help if someone becomes suspicious about me, or disgruntled. They may feel at ease opening up to you."

"Got it," said Gomez.

We need to control all aspects of our business, including the quality of the meat. We don't want anybody getting sick or we'll lose out to competitors."

"Competent, but non-compliant, and quality first, Ms. Smith. I think I can enjoy that. Especially after your comments about my age."

CHAPTER 31

Business was good. Estaban and Liliane continued to walk their clients' dogs, but for the sake of appearance, not for extra income. Dell was in control, Audrey was in control, and Gabriela was in control as well. Gomez was happy online with Jan and offline in his job. Never had things been so good for him. Elroy was Elroy, and the only thing that mattered to him was the sale: Making the sale, big or small, profitable, or not—it was all in the sale.

At the Shop Op, only Gomez and his challenged helper Mitt were allowed in the cold storage sector. Gabriela told the other employees that this was part of a new virus control policy. She explained that Gomez and Mitt had received special training on how to handle products to ensure they weren't contaminated. No questions were asked and no further explanations were needed.

The volume of sales had quadrupled since the first months of making exchanges in the parking lot. Now the parking lot sales represented only around five percent of the total, and that was only for wieners and buns. Hamburger patties, processed cheese and dairy products were all trafficked through the cold storage area under Gabriela's control and Gomez's supervision.

The problem had now become supply. Unrestricted and non-controlled jurisdictions were few and far between. Elroy explained that to up the supply, they would have to deal with more precarious sources, so called 'pop ups'—meat producers who made illegal sales by moving from location to location, hacking into the surveillance systems at each one to escape recognition. This was dangerous, because there was no synchronization between the various producers. If two or more hacked the system at the same time, it might alert the Org.

Dell and Audrey were able to follow the task force investigations and determine which suppliers were safe and which weren't, but they also found that competition was increasing and prices were falling. Heaven Number 6 meetings were increasingly devoted to the subject.

One of the problems with meeting online, the group was discovering, was that Elroy didn't participate— and Elroy had the most knowledge of the competition. In fact, Elroy worked closely with some of them on other projects, such as the boat tours in the park and 'instant avatar' mobile devices he rented by the hour for taking and receiving orders.

Audrey often asked Elroy to join them with an instant avatar, but it had to be done on a limited basis as, if used too often, limited avatar's might attract Org scrutiny.

All in all, business was getting more challenging.

Chapter 32

Gabriela, Audrey, and Elroy sat at their regular table in the bistro with hotdogs and beer. Gabriela limited herself to one of each, and considered imbibing in these things as a special treat. She was more interested in the business end of what they were doing than the gustative pleasures. Conversely, Audrey and Elroy often had more than one hotdog and always had more than one beer.

Gabriela started the meeting, "So, the market price for wieners is down 10 percent and processed foods are down an average of 15 percent. We're looking at less for all of us."

"We still have the best distribution system of anyone. Shop Op is stable and reliable," said Audrey. "It's easy for ambulant vendors to cut prices, but there's no way they can do the volume that we do."

"Not unless they are under the control of a kingpin," said Elroy. "It's never been proven, but there are rumors that the same groups that used to control the cocaine trade before it was declared an essential wellbeing substance and put under Org control are now into processed food and sugar distribution. They could be dealing in meat products too."

Gabriela looked at Audrey, "If that's true, then we have a big, long term problem. They will have a level of sophistication and a network well beyond what we have. We're going to have to be careful, because they probably already know more about us that we know about them."

Audrey leaned back and smiled. "Listen, if they are as well organized as that, and they know more about us than we know about them, then maybe they would be able to see the possibilities of working together. A price war doesn't do anyone any good, and undermining each other will eventually wake up the Org. If we attract Org attention, then we'll need to put even more sophisticated measures in place."

She turned to Elroy. "Elroy, if you know these guys, and the rumours are true, see if you can get me a meeting. Maybe we can come to some sort of agreement with them."

"That's a good idea," said Gabriela. "Do you want me to join you in that meeting?"

"That might be a good idea."

"Okay," said Elroy. "I'll scout around. I think I know who we have to speak to."

"Great," said Audrey. "That's settled then. I'm going to have another beer."

CHAPTER 33

Gabriela and Audrey went into a building designated for aged and challenged. They were there to meet a man Elroy had suggested they talk to—their competition. Gabriela acted the part of assistant to the challenged Audrey, while Audrey moved slowly past the facial cameras, pushing her walker, her protective head gear firmly in place.

At the reception desk, they asked for Mr. Sharp and the AI responder replied that Mr. Sharp was in 606. They took the elevator up to the sixth floor and knocked on Mr. Sharp's door.

A weight enhanced, aged man sat in a wheel chair at the window opposite the door. He said, "Come in. I've been waiting for you. I presume you are Audrey Hamilton and Gabriela Smith. Welcome."

"Thank you, Mr. Sharp, for meeting with us," said Audrey.

"Call me Benny."

"Well, Benny," said Audrey. "Elroy, who I believe you know, gave us your name as a person we should speak to about our mutual concerns."

"How do you know Elroy?" asked Benny

"I've known Elroy most of my life," said Audrey. "Gabriela here has known Elroy for about a year, since she became our associate. How about you?"

"I've known Elroy for a while. We do a boat business in the park. We share customers and cooperate on other issues. He's a good guy."

"How do you manage a boat business?" asked Gabriela, looking at a highly challenged male, who clearly was not very mobile. "Isn't that a highly physical job?"

"Easy, I'm very flexible," said Benny. Then he unzipped his fat suit and pulled off some masking that aged him. In front of them was no longer an aged, weight enhanced, mobility challenged old man, but a well weighted, vigorous, middle-aged male-identified person. "Image is very important, and the best image is the underestimated competency image—right?" he asked, looking directly at Audrey.

Audrey laughed, "Right, underestimated and invisible—I try to live by that philosophy."

"I guess I'm the odd person out in this one," said Gabriela.

"You're too physically imposing," Audrey said to her. "It wouldn't work for you," said Audrey. "However, it is a special skill to be able to create fear right off the bat, and you are able to do that." She turned back to Benny and said, "I think, Benny, you would agree with me on that. I'm sure you have a few on your team who are imposing."

"You're right," he said, "We all have a role to play: The unassuming guy, the numbers person on the autistic spectrum, the bully, the diplomat, the joker... The question is knowing who should *play* what role. It's not always easy."

There was silence for a moment, and then Audrey said, "So, Benny … We're both into selling illegals, you through ambulant vendors and us through a distribution system. At least that's how Elroy laid it out."

"Elroy is right. He's a good observer, and like I said, we've worked together on the boat tours and a few other things besides. I trust Elroy, you trust Elroy, so we can at least chat and see what could be mutually beneficial."

"Gabriela has some ideas on how we can work together."

"Excuse me, but I haven't offered you anything to drink," said Benny. "Can I offer you something? I've wine, beer, coffee, juice—with sugar added," said Benny with a smile.

"Coffee would be great," said Gabriela

"A beer for me," said Audrey. "I need the protein."

Benny got up and went to the fridge to get the beer. Then he poured a cup of coffee for Gabriela and one for himself. "Okay, Gabriela, I'm listening," he said.

"The way we see it, we're competing over the same suppliers and clients. Some are loyal to us and some are loyal to you. They are all getting their product, but they don't consistently get their ordered amounts at the same cost. We need to stabilize our business so our suppliers have regular, manageable orders and our clients receive their products on time and at a reasonable, set price."

Benny nodded, interested.

"We can ensure an increase in volume and profit by taking advantage of what the other does best. I'm suggesting *we* handle all the suppliers and, for a small percentage, your ambulant vendors come to Shop Op to receive the product. That way we know exactly who comes and goes and we can adjust their localization history and facials so the Org can't track them. For compensation, you can take a percentage off the deliveries to our clients. My calculations suggest that we can increase profit by 10 to 20 percent without increasing prices. And it will reduce Org tracking danger to near zero."

Then Gabriela looked at Audrey. "Should I mention the task force?" she asked.

"Go ahead."

"Audrey is plugged into all Org task force investigations. Without divulging any names, we have an in at the Org. As a matter of fact, I was a senior manager at the Org not so long ago, and I know exactly what their strengths and weaknesses are."

Benny looked impressed. "Well, I would say we have a deal in principal—we just have to work out the details," he said. Then he added, "You do realize that we are not the only game in town and this little joint venture might not please some people? I'm sure we can deal with it, but I just wanted to point that out."

"I understand," said Audrey. "But the reality is that we are just combining our suppliers and clients under one roof for more and better service. We are open to helping others, too … for a certain percentage."

Benny thought a little, "So we'd be like what they used to call a 'cartel' back in the old illegal drug days?"

"Yeah, something like that," said Audrey. "I think they used to call it a syndicate too, in some places."

"Well then let's toast to it," said Benny.

The three toasted and then sat at the table in silence. Gabriela was deep in thought as to how to organize and identify additional traffic, and keep track of the numbers. Audrey was making calculations about currency and surveillance technology. Benny was thinking about how he would deal with other competition; would he bring them in on the action or squeeze them out? There were a lot of decisions to be made.

CHAPTER 34

Gabriela ran a tight ship at Shop Op. Her pay increase percentage permitted her to upgrade her lifestyle to even beyond what it was when she was senior manager at Org. She was also winning the custody battle with her ex, as she was able to spoil Sarah just enough to make her weeks at her mother's more entertaining than at her father's.

Gabriela felt a little guilty concerning her actions in this regard, but for a while she had been disadvantaged, and she justified it as catch up.

She had also decided to create another avatar and join an Otherlife program, a mixture of neuro-consciousness and Buddhist universal consciousness. Her avatar was an entity that communicated with other entities in the pursuit of knowledge and neuro-expansion. Truthfully, however, preferred her avatar Annie in Heaven Number 6. It was more entertaining and less tedious.

Gabriela had not spoken to Audrey about her online life, and for good reason. She was beginning to see that she had to get more control over her situation, both online and offline. She didn't have the coding and tech skills Audrey and Elroy had and she felt like she needed to find someone who did to work on her behalf so she would be on an equal footing with them—and, if need be, more independent.

Bill Sittler had a son who was designated as highly data driven, on the autistic spectrum and socially challenged. Gabriela had heard he was technically apt in the world of bits and qbits. Bill himself was almost the direct opposite of his son but, while Gabriela found him to be a little overbearing in his social interactions, he got along well with the employees. As Gomez was fond of saying, he wasn't so bad once you get used to him. And Bill's son, Jon, sounded like he might be exactly who Gabriela was looking for. It was certainly worth finding out.

CHAPTER 35

"Mr. Sittler, may I join you?" asked Gabriela. She had picked up a coffee in the lunch room and was now standing at the table where Bill sat, biting into his tofu sandwich.

"Yes, of course, Ms. Smith," he said.

Bill looked worried and sat up straight. Ms. Smith rarely ate with staff, and this was the first time she had joined him when he was alone. Had he done something wrong? Was he about to be fired or reassigned?

"Well, Mr. Sittler … It feels so good just to relax once in a while. How about we use our first names when we're on our breaks—after all we've been working together for quite some time now. Maybe I've been a little too formal in my relationship with the employees. I'd like to change that a little."

"No problem, Ms. Smith."

"Gabriela, Bill—Gabriela."

"Gabriela," said Bill with a nervous smile.

"So, how's the family, Bill? What's your son's name again—Jack, or John?"

"Jon," he said proudly. "And he's okay—same as usual. He spends all his time on his computer, doing who knows what."

"I know what you mean. My daughter Sarah is the same. Her life, like that of so many others, is mostly online. We eat together sometimes, and occasionally I force her to go for a walk in the park with me, but that's about it. I don't know who her online persona is, or whether she's in Afterlife or Otherlife."

Bill started to warm up to the conversation. "I wish Jon was online, but unfortunately he seems interested only in creating apps and the like. Sometimes I'm afraid he's going to hack the wrong place and get us into trouble. I once caught him changing his profile so the facial and audio recognized him as someone else."

Bill suddenly felt a little uncomfortable—had he said too much? He quickly added, "I made him promise not to do that again. I explained the possible repercussions."

Gabriela had just heard what she wanted to hear. This was it, exactly what she was looking for. She was certain that Jon was what used to be called an 'Asperger genius' or a 'highly functioning autistic'. She needed him. He was an Audrey that wasn't purpose driven—and she could provide the purpose.

"I'm getting another coffee, Bill," she said, "would you like one?"

"Yes, thank you Gabriela, that would be great." If he was surprised at how nice she was being, he didn't show it.

Gabriela went to the coffee machine and returned with two coffees. "You know, Bill, I just had a thought. If you don't think it will work, no problem—but maybe Jon can help here at Shop Op."

"What do you mean? Jon has never been able to keep a job. At the last one, he only had to separate the reusable from the recyclable at a container depot, and he couldn't do that."

"He likes to code, create apps, work out digital and quantum problems—right? Maybe he has been under-utilized and has just been doing the wrong thing. The thing is, Bill, we need someone here at Shop Op to create better applications, synchronize our data, and generally make things run better. He might have the skills we're looking for. What do you think, Bill?"

"I suppose I could ask him … and if you would give him a chance, that would be great. I really appreciate that Ms. Smith—I mean Gabriela. I have to say, I got the wrong impression of you at our first meeting. I didn't see the human side of you. We don't often see people who are willing to help offline."

"Bill, I have a daughter and you have a son. I can empathize with you. So let's give it a try. Talk to Jon and have him meet with me. Hopefully, everything will work out for all of us. Also Bill, you've been doing a great job here. I've decided to put you in charge of the front end of Shop Op. You'll manage employees, payouts, produce—the whole works. Gomez will take care of the back end, the docks, storage and so on. There will be a pay raise, of course."

"I don't know what to say, Gabriela. You won't regret it—I'll do a bang-up job."

"You know, Bill, I think we work well together. We both have a knack of looking for mutual benefits when doing a job. That's how a business runs well. By the way, that sandwich looks like it could use a piece of ham in it. But that would be illegal, wouldn't it—real ham from a real pig?"

"Of course, Gabriela. I wouldn't do that to Shop Op."

"Listen Bill, I haven't tasted real meat for a long time. I wouldn't be against it if you, or anyone, indulged in it from time to time."

Bill looked at Gabriela, but said nothing. He had memories of real beef, and real ham with real eggs. It had been a while ... *but wouldn't it be nice*, he thought?

"That's big of you, Gabriela," he said.

"Well, maybe we can work something out there too. Anyway, talk to Jon and tell him to come and see me."

CHAPTER 36

Shop Op was now doing more business in illegals and restricted products than it was in organic, whole food certified substances, but Gabriela and Audrey could both see potential problems up ahead. They needed an avant-garde, health-oriented branding change.

Business-minded Gabriela asked questions for economic reasons. One was, why did Shop Op need a parking lot? Individual cars were a throwback to an old mentality.

"Listen Audrey," she said one day. "The trunk to trunk transfers have been completely replaced by dock in and dock out. The regulars and legal substances are bringing in less and less of our income, and almost all of that goes to the Org and Shop Op headquarters."

"You're right, Gabriela, but a steady stream of income to headquarters keeps them from auditing our store."

"Okay, but what if we were to go strictly person-mobile, catering only to bicycle traffic, pedestrians and challenged in mobile transporters. What if we said, 'no cars, whether they be hybrid, electric, hydrogen or whatever'? We can brand ourselves as a healthy environment catering to the healthy. And allowing mobile transporters for the challenged will make it inclusive—nobody would dare oppose that."

"Sounds good, what's your idea?"

"My idea is that we tear up the parking lot and plant vegetables, herbs, marijuana, coca plants and poppies. The big volume clients use the docks in and out at the back."

"Wow, I like it!" said Audrey. "It's perfect. We add all-natural essentials and medicinals. There is a market for that, for sure. It'll pay and be the perfect cover too."

"And at certain times of the year, customers will be invited to come and pick their own produce. We can have our own app for the payment."

"And we can have a special place where they can dry their own leaves, if they're buying herbs or marijuana!" added Audrey. "But building an app for that could be a problem—I don't have the time to put into it."

"I think I can solve that problem. I have a good resource working for us at Shop Op. He is capable of building the necessary apps and control systems, plus keeping them from Org eyes. I've been working with him on streamlining the accounts systems, and supplier controls, among other things. Maybe you've seen an improvement lately in the numbers delivery?"

"I thought things seemed different," Audrey said. "That's good—but can he be trusted?"

"I believe so. He's well into the socially challenged aspect on the autism spectrum—and I mean for *real*, not fabricated like yours. His name is Jon and he's Bill Sittler's son."

"Okay, but keep an eye on him anyway, and show me his programs when they are developed. I'll just check for any weaknesses."

"No problem. So it's a go for the new branding and set up?"

"It's a go. I'll inform Benny and Elroy about the changes, just so nobody feels like they're out of the loop," Audrey said.

"Maybe let Dell know too, so he can work with Jon if the need arises."

"Okay. And we'll have a meeting in Heaven Number 6 with the gang and bring everyone up to date."

"Your favourite server, Annie, will be there," Gabriela said. "I might tone it down a little so you can make sure everyone is on the right page—I know I got a little snappy the last time."

Then Gabriela took on a more serious tone and leaned in toward Audrey, "Audrey, I want to talk to you about something," she said.

"Go ahead, Gabriela. Is something wrong?"

"What about Benny? I'm just wondering what his role is. I know he had his ambulant vendors and was in with Elroy, but what is his use to us, exactly?"

Audrey looked at Gabriela in surprise. It was true that she had thought about Benny's cut and the relatively little effort he put into the operation. While his original ambulant vendors were still there and operating, he hadn't brought in any new business and yet his percentage was on the total business.

"What are you suggesting, Gabriela?" Audrey asked.

"I'm not suggesting anything. I'm just wondering what his purpose is. Gomez earns his cut, Elroy makes his, even Bill Sittler is more useful to us than Benny, and he doesn't know the role he plays … although I suspect he knows what's going on. He just prefers to ignore it."

"Listen, I'll think about it. Maybe I'll get him to do a little promo and increase his side of the business."

"It's too bad he wasn't really challenged and then we could ignore him," said Gabriela. She smiled slightly and said, "You could pull a Gabriela on him—it certainly got *me* out of your hair."

"Maybe I'll have a talk with Dell and see if I can get him certified mentally challenged with second stage dementia. We could have the Org put him in a special unit that only allows designated visitors and has a no-exit restriction. You could be his only designated visitor," joked Audrey.

"I know we're just joking, but in reality that might not be such a bad plan," said Gabriela

Gabriela was coming up with ideas that seemed a little extreme to Audrey, and it bothered her. It's true that Benny was becoming a weight on the operation, but there was a question of loyalty. Maybe Gabriela didn't see it that way because of how she had lost her status at the Org.

As if reading Audrey's mind, Gabriela said, "Listen, Audrey, forget it. There's no harm in having Benny onboard and we had an agreement with him that we should honor."

Then she got up and left. She had to get back to Shop Op and see where Jon was with his hacking. He was making good progress in putting her back in the driver's seat. On her instruction, he'd managed to find the disappeared Ms. Smith files without anyone noticing. The plan would be executed in three quick movements, done simultaneously before Audrey could react or even understand what was happening.

Tit for tat, thought Gabriela.

CHAPTER 37

Gabriela liked and had great esteem for Audrey; actually, she really liked the whole espresso gang. And why not? They were unordinary and they were good at being unordinary.

But what Gabriela really liked was control and power. *I will continue to work with them all,* she thought. *But I'm getting back in the driver's seat. I want my old job, my new friends, but mostly I want control.*

Gabriela knew she had to act fast if her plan was to work. She'd learned from experience that to fool Audrey she had to be precise and quick.

She had everything in place and she had a go-forward plan to streamline the business—her business. Benny would be gone. He was definitely dead weight and too old school and in this environment she needed smarts, not muscle. Jon would provide the digital control from the Org side, and Audrey would handle the digital control outside the Org.

It would be the perfect setup. She would be in control both online and offline. There would be a little frustration and some hard feelings at first, but eventually everyone would see the advantages.

Gabriela set the plan into action.

Two men in protective clothing and masks stood next to a mobile hospital bed kitted out with wheels and straps in front of an apartment door. They knocked several times and when they got no response, they took out a key and opened it.

"Benjamin Sharp—are you Benjamin Sharp?" they asked as they barged in.

"Yes? What do you gentlemen want—and how did you open my door?" Benny yelped before realizing what was going on. "You bastards! Fuckers! I was warned they would want me out!"

The men didn't respond. They simply approached Benny, gave him a shot in the arm, put him on the bed, strapped him in, and left with an unconscious Benny, down the elevator and out the front door. No one noticed as Benny was put in an ambulance and taken away, and even if they had, it was not unusual, as he was weight and mobility challenged and ripe for a health failure of some sort.

Dell arrived at his office and tried to enter his code. It wasn't working. He could see Jon Sittler through the window. Dell motioned him to open the door. Jon simply ignored him and continued working.

Dell went to the reception area. "Can we help you Mr. Gabo?" asked the female-identified at the desk.

"My code doesn't seem to work for the office and conference room."

"I'm sorry Mr. Gabo, but talkers don't have codes to the door. You must wait until you are summoned. Those are the rules, Mr. Gabo."

Dell felt a buzz in his pocket and checked his mobile, 'meet in Heaven Number 6'.

He didn't know who it was from, but he was quick to clue in to the fact that he'd apparently been demoted. He decided to head back to his apartment before he went online. Whatever was going down, he wanted to be sitting down for it.

Audrey was sitting in her favourite chair in the vintage clothing store with a cup of double espresso when she received the same message, 'meet in Heaven Number 6 and bring Elroy as Punk'. Estaban, Liliane and Gomez all received the same message, and wondered, *what is happening?*

About half an hour after the message went out, Lyle, Max, Hector, Walrus, Kata, and Punk were all in Heaven Number 6 in their regular espresso bar. The only one missing was Jan. They sat looking at each other, then at Lyle, wondering if he could explain what was going on. Lyle said nothing.

Annie came to the table to take their orders. "How about a round of our best vintage wine for everyone? It's on the house."

"Sounds good," said Lyle. "You wouldn't know why we are here, would you Annie?"

"Let's start with the wine first," said Annie overly cheerfully as she left the table to get the wine and glasses. She was back before they had a chance to discuss her attitude.

Annie grabbed a chair and sat down with the gang. "I guess you are all wondering why you are here. If you haven't yet figured it out, I sent the message you all got today. I sent it because I want to inform you of some changes."

"Changes to what?" asked Max.

"Changes to the structure of our organization, right Annie?" said Lyle dryly.

"Right, Lyle!" said Annie, acknowledging how quickly Lyle/Audrey understood.

"To begin with, I am going to take this organization to a higher level, and if I asked you to come here it's because there is a place for each and every one of you in this new model."

"But *you* will be in charge," said Lyle. "In other words this is a takeover—the Queen is dead, long live the Queen. Am I right?"

Annie laughed, while the others just looked back and forth between Annie and Lyle with a stunned look on their faces.

"Something like that," said Annie, pouring each of them more wine. "But please understand that this is about improving our business, not taking away rights and privileges. I just know that I'm the right person to run the show."

No one said anything, not even Lyle.

"Here's how it's going to be," said Annie. "This is not a hostile takeover, it's just a takeover. I understand it will be hard to adjust to in the beginning, but I am really going to get this business off the ground. We will continue our regular meetings, here online, and in the bistro offline. Elroy you will be Punk in Heaven Number 6 from now on."

"Punk, hey? What the hell, it will add more spice to my existence," Elroy said.

"We will be expanding our operation. Punk, you will take over Benny's job. Hector and Walrus, you will be use your connections in the non-tech sector—your dog walking clients, for example—to expand our consumer base. Audrey you will be in charge of offline operations such as suppliers, clients, locations, and any digital coordination between the Org and our business. Jon Sittler is our man in the Org for the digital. Dell you will coordinate clients and make sure everyone is happy. You're a good talker listener and we need you doing that. Max will help you with that."

The group nodded slowly, unsure but in no position to argue. Gabriela added, "I will be in charge of the overall operation and will make sure we are free of interference from the Org. Someone has to be able to deal with cracks and weaknesses and ensure we're a strong outfit."

She looked at the assembled group and they looked back at her, clearly surprised but also pleased with her vision.

"That's it, that's all folks—enjoy your wine and I'll leave you to discuss and decide if you're in or out," said Gabriela as she got up and started clearing tables.

CHAPTER 38

Gabriela entered the Org office building dressed in suit and tie.

"Good morning, Ms. Smith."

"Good Morning, Jeb. How are you today?"

"Just fine. Your people are waiting for you in the conference room."

Gabriela headed to the elevator. She assumed her meeting would be on the twelfth floor, in her old office, which until recently had been occupied by Dell. So far, so good—her day was going exactly as planned. She had all her professional stats and connections back, including her accounts. She also had full access to, and control of, her Shop Op file. Bill would be able to manage the Shop Op in her absence until Max and Audrey were up to speed, and Jon was providing the necessary tech support.

Mr. Fortin and Mr. Wang greeted her as she entered the office.

"Good morning, gentlemen," she said. "Could you send me the updated Afterlife and Otherlife files? I need to look at some of changes in the last 24 hours. Also, I'd like an update on the task force Mr. Sanchez is running."

"We'll get them to you right away, Ms. Smith."

"Are Mr. Sanchez and Ms. Singh in the conference room?"

"Yes, they're there waiting for you with the information you requested."

Gabriela went into her office, looked out the window and checked her messages. Then she picked up a coffee at the newly installed espresso machine and made her way to the conference room.

"Good morning, Mr. Sanchez. Good morning, Ms. Singh."

"Good morning Ms. Smith. We're ready to report."

"Good," she said. "I'd like to introduce you to Jon Sittler. He will be assisting me. Make sure he has access to everything he might need. If he asks for something, treat it as if it was a request from me."

CHAPTER 39

Dell, Gomez, Elroy, Estaban, Liliane and Audrey met in their usual bistro later that day. They were sitting around their table by the window, each with a pint of dark beer in front of them.

"Who wants to start?" asked Audrey taking a huge gulp of beer.

"Did we ever get screwed!" said Dell taking a sip, followed by a fist full of peanuts. "I never saw that coming. Can you believe it? I'm not sure I like my role, or if I even understand it. I'm supposed to listen and make sure everything is cool. How do I know when it's cool? I think I'd prefer to be just a plain talker."

"It's kind of funny, really," said Gomez. "We got rid of Ms. Smith, just to get Gabriela. And I'm wondering about Jan. Will she change or stay the same?"

"Don't worry Gomez," said Audrey, "Jan will stay the same. Gabriela prefers being Annie and has no reason to be Jan, or to upset you,"

"Well," said Elroy, "look on the bright side— the bistro still has peanuts, pure meat hotdogs, and hamburgers. The boat tours on the lake are still ours, and independent. The only downside for me is that I'm taking over Benny's role, so life is a little more complicated."

"What about you, Audrey?"

"What can I say?" Audrey said, taking another sip of her beer. "She outplayed us. She pulled off our own stunt and essentially put us back where we were, but with more experience and a profitable little business. She will no doubt be successful in expanding and increasing the business, but I expect our cut will drop as a percentage in time. However, I have no doubt the money we make will increase in absolute terms. We can help her or not. I'm pretty sure if we decide not to join her, she will leave us be."

"So you say we go along, join her, or not?" asked Liliane.

"I'm thinking I'm going to join her," said Audrey. "Her plan is logical and she is trying to make good use of all our talents, whether we can see it or not."

"I think we're all with you, Audrey," said Elroy and the others nodded in the affirmative. They were a team and they would stick together.

Audrey stood up and put her beer mug high in the air, "Listen, what she is creating will be huge. It's structured and it's designed to keep out the competition. She wants to be the only player on the scene. In other words it's an Org, an *illicit* Org.

Elroy scratched his chin. "An illicit Org that we helped build," he said.

"Yes," said Audrey. "But remember, gang, we're *disturbers*. We play the system, and we will play this system too. We will take on our roles, but we will watch for the weaknesses and work it in our favour. An org is an org, whether legal or illegal. Inevitably it will over-structure and bureaucratize itself."

"Let's drink to that," yelled Gomez,

"To disturbing, and the opportunities that lie ahead," shouted Dell.

"And to fun!" screamed Audrey

Manufactured by Amazon.ca
Bolton, ON